DOC SAVAGE'S AMAZING CREW

William Harper Littlejohn, the bespectacled scientist who was the world's greatest living expert on geology and archaeology.

Colonel John Renwick, "Renny," his favorite sport was pounding his massive fists through heavy, paneled doors.

Lieutenant Colonel Andrew Blodgett Mayfair, "Monk," only a few inches over five feet tall, and yet over 260 pounds. His brutish exterior concealed the mind of a great scientist.

Major Thomas J. Roberts, "Long Tom," was the physical weakling of the crowd, but a genius at electricity.

Brigadier General Theodore Marley Brooks, slender and waspy, he was never without his ominous, black sword cane.

WITH THEIR LEADER, THEY WOULD GO
ANYWHERE, FIGHT ANYONE, DARE EVERYTHING—
SEEKING EXCITEMENT AND PERILOUS ADVENTURE!

THE
SEA ANGEL

A DOC SAVAGE ADVENTURE
BY KENNETH ROBESON

BANTAM BOOKS · TORONTO · NEW YORK · LONDON
A NATIONAL GENERAL COMPANY

THE SEA ANGEL

*A Bantam Book / published by arrangement with
The Condé Nast Publications Inc.*

PRINTING HISTORY

Originally published in DOC SAVAGE *Magazine November 1937
Bantam edition published June 1970*

*Bantam Books are published by Bantam Books, Inc., a National
General company. Its trade-mark, consisting of the words "Bantam
Books" and the portrayal of a bantam, is registered in the United
States Patent Office and in other countries. Marca Registrada.
Bantam Books, Inc., 666 Fifth Avenue, New York, N.Y. 10019.*

PRINTED IN THE UNITED STATES OF AMERICA

CONTENTS

THE SEA ANGEL

Chapter I

THE AMAZING REDSKINS

HE was a peaceful old gentleman who was scared out of his wits. Peaceful-looking, that is. His hair was white, and his skin was as soft and pink as a baby's even if it did have wrinkles in it.

He was frightened. As terrified and as full of cold, horrible suspense as a man watching a black widow spider crawl down his arm.

The scared old man was getting out of an automobile in front of the main entrance to the Museum of Natural History. The automobile was one equipped with armor plate and special glass. Another automobile had driven up to the museum entrance ahead of it. Still another had followed behind. These two escort cars were full of gentlemen with guns in their pockets, suspicion in their eyes, and detective badges—private and police—on their clothing.

Before the old gentleman stirred from his car, the guards scattered over the sidewalk and into the museum, looking around, then signaled discreetly that it was safe.

Having observed nobody suspicious inside the museum, the burly man in charge of the guards came out to report to the old gentleman.

"Coast looks clear," he said. "But, Mr. Quietman, it would make it a lot simpler if we had some idea of just who is threatening you. Who is this Sea Angel?"

The old gentleman—Leander L. Quietman, philanthropist, patron of arts, beloved old gentleman who gave dollar bills to poor newsboys, according to the newspapers—shrugged and looked exasperated.

"I've told you I do not know!" he said. "It—the thing—your job is to protect me from anything. *Anything!* Now, I am going in to have a look at the exhibit of the Calhugi Indians which I am presenting to the museum."

As he entered the museum, Quietman looked just a bit more scared than any man should be who does not know what he is scared of, except that it was a telephone voice calling itself the "Sea Angel."

THE Calhugi Indian exhibit was located in an alcove off the enormous third-floor hall which contained exhibits of other tribes of American, Canadian and Alaskan Indians. There was not a single visitor or spectator in the room. The reason for this was simple: It was seven o'clock in the morning, and the museum was not yet open to visitors.

Leander L. Quietman, after having a guard go ahead to make sure the place was empty of human presence, said, "You men may wait for me outside if you wish. I prefer to admire this alone."

Then he walked toward the exhibit which he was donating.

The bodyguards loafed outside the door and indulged in their favorite pastime of trying to figure out who or what was menacing Leander L. Quietman.

Meanwhile, Leander L. Quietman was walking toward his Calhugi Indian exhibit, which was at the far end of the hall. The Calhugi Indians were probably as little-known aborigines as ever chased a buffalo or paddled a birch-bark canoe.

Quietman drew a breath of admiration when he saw his exhibit, only just completed by the finest restoration artists in the business. Experts in working with wax.

It consisted of a sod house shaped like a beehive. At one side of the house stood a small herd of six shaggy ponies. On one of these ponies sat a squat, enormously thick and broad Indian.

This Indian had an amazing set of muscles, which was probably fortunate, because he did not look as if he could possibly have many brains. Other Calhugi savages were seated, cross-legged, around a camp fire, along with their squaws. They were engaged in arrow-making and other pursuits.

Quietman heaved another sigh of admiration. He stepped under the velvet rope surrounding the exhibit and advanced for a closer look at a wax Calhugi Indian, who was making a tomahawk.

"A marvelous work of art!" gasped Leander L. Quietman, after a close look. "A beautiful specimen of the human race!"

"My mother always thought so, too," said the Calhugi brave, who was supposed to be made of wax.

The next instant, he had Quietman by the throat and had lifted his tomahawk.

"One peep," he said, "and I'll tomahawk you plenty!"

Poor old Leander L. Quietman became pale, and began to shake.

The Calhugi Indian sitting on the wax pony got off. His legs were stiff, and he staggered about ludicrously.

"Damn this razorback horse!" he groaned.

Several more of the supposedly wax redskins now got up, and two came out of the sod beehive. One of these carried a rope ladder.

The squat, muscular fellow who had been on the horse—he had an enormous stomach of the type commonly called pot-belly—now took charge.

"The window," he said. "And no more wise cracks. Them bodyguards may hear us."

"O. K., Boscoe," the fake Indians agreed, and grabbed Leander L. Quietman.

"W-what does this m-mean?" Quietman gulped.

"It means," said the tubby "Boscoe," "that we had to try this crazy gag to get our hands on you. You didn't think that because you walked around in a swarm of cops and body-guards we wouldn't get you, did you? Grabbing you is the only way to save you from the Sea Angel."

Quietman choked, "S-saving me f-from the Sea Angel?"

"Believe it or not, and strange as it seems," Boscoe agreed.

Quietman moaned, "Y-you are m-making a mistake!"

"The hell we are!" Boscoe grinned.

The men proceeded with their saving. They taped Quietman's lips, fastened his wrists with wider tape, then led him to a window. One opened the window. Tying Quietman to an end of the rope ladder, they lowered him.

During this operation, Boscoe went back to the Calhugi Indian exhibit and pilfered. He stuffed his pockets with stone knives, flint arrowheads and several pairs of moccasins.

Boscoe seemed to forget everything else in his absorption with the looting. He grabbed two or three bows, two toma-hawks, then began to tuck arrows under an arm. He added a long spear. Indeed, he seemed bent on taking everything in sight.

Several of the men were now down the ladder, and they had untied old Leander L. Quietman and were holding him. The others descended. Boscoe was last.

Boscoe's descent was something of burlesque comedy. He had stuffed his Indian garments with everything they would hold, and had both arms full, which left no hands free to handle the rope ladder.

It was with the greatest reluctance that he surrendered an armload of his loot, and climbed down.

"Whatcha gonna do with that stuff?" a man gritted.

"Oh, I dunno," Boscoe said vaguely. "I'll think of something."

THE Museum of Natural History originally started with one building, and others were added. There are alleyways and courts between these structures. The men had descended into one of the courts, from which an alley led to a side street.

They got in motion, two of them guiding Leander L. Quietman.

Boscoe had his difficulties. He dropped an arrow, stooped to pick it up, and lost two moccasins. He progressed in this fashion, bobbing along after the others, but leaving a trail of erstwhile Calhugi belongings. He groaned in agony as he saw his loot dwindling.

This obviously tickled his companions. They grinned widely.

Then their grins faded.

A most remarkable-looking man had appeared in front of them.

Chapter II

THE SEA ANGEL

STANDING on pedestals here and there inside that part of the museum devoted to sculpture were a number of bronze statues of ancient athletes who had legendary strength.

This stranger was like that. He might as readily have been one of the statues come to life, as the other men had lately been Calhugi Indians. He was, however, attired in a neat, brown civilian suit, and there was no make-up on his skin to make it resemble bronze, whereas the others had their hides painted a coppery red.

Nothing happened for some moments. The fake redskins looked at the man they had met.

Boscoe said quickly, "Watch it, guys, watch it! Daniel in the lion's den didn't have anything on us!"

"One side, bronze guy!" a man snarled. "Or we'll take you plenty!"

"You apes!" Boscoe growled. "Do you know who this guy——"

Boscoe did not finish. The action started. A man pointed his pistol at the bronze giant. There was blurred motion, and the bronze giant was not where he had been; and two men were flat on their backs, kicking their legs like flies and trying to figure out just what had happened.

Poor old Leander L. Quietman had been dropped on the hard cement alley pavement. The men who had held him leaped to the attack.

A man drew a gun. "Get 'em up!"

"Nix!" Boscoe barked anxiously.

The next instant, as if by some miraculous legerdemain, the bronze man had secured the gun. He pointed it at the sky, pulled the trigger. A mousetrap would have made more noise. The pistol was not loaded.

Boscoe groaned, "Now he knows our guns are empty!"

If the fact that a gang of men staging a kidnaping carried

unloaded guns amazed the bronze giant, he did not show emotion about it.

The fight continued. It became obvious the unbelievable was going to happen. The mountain was coming to Mahomet, water would run uphill. One amazing bronze man was going to whip the whole gang!

Then, and the very suddenness of it was incredibly weird, men seemed to freeze where they stood. They had been jumping about wildly, striking, trying to get clear of their Nemesis. They stiffened. It was as if they were a movie which had been stopped at one scene. They seemed scarcely to breathe, until finally, Boscoe lifted a thick arm slowly and pointed.

"The Sea Angel!" he croaked.

THE bronze man—Doc Savage—whirled and saw it.

Fantastic thing. An incredible thing. Had it been night, the thing might have been a bit more believable.

Eight feet might be the height of the incredible creature. That, though, was a guess. It was frilly around the edges. It was half as wide as high. It had a thick part for a body. It had triangular wings, two of them, and these ran to a point; and from these dangled black ropelike arms, eight or ten feet long. Each arm terminated in a black ball a little smaller than a baseball.

Silver was the creature's color. The slick silver of a fish. But there were black markings—the edges of the thing, and the arms.

As it stood there, it did bear some resemblance to an angel.

It had a mouth. This was evident when the mouth opened and showed a jet-black gullet. The mouth was large enough to take a beer keg, with only a little stretching.

Boscoe croaked, "Boys, we're in a predicament now!"

Doc Savage lunged for the silver monstrosity. He was lightning on his feet.

But the Sea Angel was lightning doubled. One of the black arms whipped forward, and the long, black rope came around like a blacksnake whip.

Doc dodged, and the dark ball barely touched him. But the touch had an incredible effect: He felt it from head to foot. Not pain. Something else. Shock. Agony.

The bronze man stumbled back, was clear when the other arm struck. He kept moving, reached old Leander Quietman, scooped him up.

It became evident that there was no way out of the alley

and court. But in a corner was a small brick box of a building, the door open, a key in the lock. Tools, lawn mowers, were inside.

Doc whipped to the shed, popped Leander Quietman inside, and closed the door. He turned the key in the lock, then took the key out.

Doc got close to the brick wall. He shoved the key into a cranny between the bricks, twisted, and broke it so that it would never open the little tool cubicle again.

The strange creature, the Sea Angel, glided to the tool house, fluttered about it a moment. It could not get in. It made no sound.

Boscoe and his men ran. They ran as if getting away from there was the nicest thing they had ever been able to do.

THE Sea Angel advanced on Doc Savage. The bronze man dipped into his clothing and brought out a small gas grenade. He hurled it. The thing broke against the monster, poured out tear gas.

The tear gas had absolutely no effect, except that it made it necessary for the bronze man to get away immediately. He managed to do it by a wild rush.

Doc got out of the alley and onto a side street.

Boscoe and his men were in two cars, leaving rapidly.

A young woman stood on the sidewalk. An unusually tall and attractive young woman, who was staring in wonder at the goings-on.

Suddenly she screamed, whirled, ran.

She had seen, of course, the Sea Angel. The thing was following Doc Savage.

Doc ran swiftly. Construction work was being done on a near-by street, under the elevated railway. The bronze man made for the loose bricks, and when he reached them, he picked one up, and let fly.

The brick struck squarely. And the monster wavered for an instant, driven off balance. Doc picked up more bricks. The incredible apparition retreated swiftly.

A taxicab came cruising around the corner, and the day-dreaming driver saw the silver-and-black creature. He gave a violent start and hung his amazed face out a window.

One of the monster's strange, black feelers snaked out and barely touched the driver's elbow. The hackman shrieked. Screeched as if he had lost the arm. And he fed his cab gears and gas.

The monster leaped, and got onto the cab. Not onto the running board, but across the top, great flipperlike wings draped down on the side, the black feelers tossed up over its back.

The taxi driver saw what he had aboard. He was still shrieking when he and his machine and his fantastic passenger were lost to sight, six blocks away.

Doc Savage ran to his car, a long, powerful, plain roadster and gave chase; but the cab was gone, although he hunted over an area of many blocks before he gave up.

Doc Savage went back to the alley between the museum buildings where he had left old Leander L. Quietman.

The girl who had been such an interested observer of the excitement was not in sight. She was, it developed, concealed just inside the mouth of the alley. She showed Doc the business end of a small lady's pistol when he walked into the alley.

"You will put up your hands," she said, and shook a little.

"Miss Quietman," Doc Savage said. "Sure you are not making a mistake?"

She widened her eyes at him. "You know me?"

"You are Nancy Quietman."

She snapped, "That makes no difference! Get your hands up!"

Doc Savage appeared not to hear the order. "Changed your mind or something?"

"What do you mean?"

"It was you who asked me to try to help your grandfather, who was in trouble. You wrote me a letter."

"Oh!" Nancy Quietman lowered her gun. "You are Doc Savage! I'm sorry. I did not know you."

"I am glad," Doc told her.

She showed surprise. "Glad that any one should not recognize *you?*"

"Publicity," the bronze man said, "is very bad for any one doing such work as myself and my aids do. Now, what is your grandfather's trouble? Your letter gave no details."

"I do not know," Nancy Quietman said. "He has suddenly become terribly worried about something. He hired bodyguards, and got the police to assign detectives to guard him."

"What excuse did he give the police?"

"Merely that he was scared."

Doc questioned, "You have no other clue?"

"No," Nancy Quietman said. "Unless it is this: I heard grandfather muttering over and over, 'the twenty-third! I am to be the twenty-third!' He said it did not mean anything when I asked him about it."

She was silent, looking, at the bronze man. Finally, the girl shuddered.

"Was it real?" she asked. "Has any one ever heard of it before?"

The bronze man did not answer.

"Your grandfather?" Doc Savage asked finally.

"I found him in the tool shed," Nancy Quietman said. "He was yelling. One of the groundkeepers let him out."

"We might talk to him," Doc said, and walked into the alley between the museum buildings.

But old Leander Quietman was not there.

Some groundkeepers and a few curiosity-seekers stood around and looked puzzled.

"He left," they explained, "in a hurry."

Chapter III

THE THREAT LETTERS

Doc Savage and Nancy Quietman hurriedly entered the museum. They found the phalanx of guards blissfully unaware that anything had happened to Leander Quietman.

"Those men probably doubled back and seized him!" the girl said, and added that it was a wonder some one had not taken to stealing the New York City police stations.

Whatever the cops thought about this, they were polite enough not to say. Doc Savage and the young woman walked out on the street.

The newsboy was still there, yelling the headlines. Doc bought a paper. When he opened it, black type was big on the page.

GRAND JURY FAILS TO INDICT MAYFAIR!

———

"Awful Miscarriage of Justice," District Attorney Says.

Nancy Quietman said, "I suppose you have dismissed that man, Andrew Blodgett Mayfair, or Monk, as he is called, from your organization?"

"I have," Doc said quietly.

The girl nodded approvingly.

"It was terrible, the way he swindled that poor lawyer, Theodore Marley Brooks—Ham, as he is nicknamed," the girl said.

Nancy Quietman, in referring to the swindle mentioned in the newspapers, was talking about a scandal that had started the politicians in Washington howling, and which had turned collective Wall Street as pale as a ghost. The politicians were claiming it proved the laws governing Wall Street were too lax, and Wall Street was afraid of what the politicians would do.

Andrew Blodgett "Monk" Mayfair had cleverly swindled

Brigadier General Theodore Marley "Ham" Brooks, noted war veteran, out of three million dollars, reducing Ham to a pauper. Poor, impoverished Ham had attempted to take his own life.

On the other hand, the rapscallion Monk boasted that everything had been perfectly legal, and apparently it had, because they were still trying to get him in jail.

Doc Savage had ejected Monk from his organization and publicly branded any one who would commit such a swindle as a type of rascal which was not doing the country any good.

The method by which Monk had perpetrated his swindle on Ham was a bit too complicated in its legal aspects for an average citizen to understand.

"Your grandfather may have gone home," Doc told the girl.

"I live at grandfather's house," she said. "Would you care to accompany me there and perhaps talk with him?"

The bronze man accepted the invitation.

THE Leander L. Quietman mansion bore more resemblance to a church than to a home. It was an old-timer, and situated on an uptown eminence overlooking the Hudson River.

A butler in exactly the correct attire opened the door.

"Your grandfather just left, Miss Quietman," he said, when asked about Leander L. Quietman.

"So he got back safe!" the girl exclaimed happily.

The elderly butler adjusted his eyeglasses. "Your grandfather took his bags, miss. He asked me to tell you he might be gone for some time."

"Where did he go?"

"He didn't say, miss."

"That's queer," Nancy Quietman said, and looked worried for a few moments. Then she smiled at Doc Savage. "Would you like to have coffee with me?"

They entered a room which she explained was her grandfather's laboratory.

"Oh!" she exclaimed, looking around. "What—what——"

The desk drawers were hanging out, the papers in them birdnests of confusion. Other papers were on the floor.

"Grandfather left in a hurry!" Nancy Quietman gasped, explaining a scene that spoke for itself.

"Would you give me your permission to make an investigation, Miss Quietman?" Doc Savage asked quietly.

"You think something is wrong?"

"Manifestly," Doc said. "First, the call for bodyguards, then the attempted kidnaping, now this."

"Go ahead with your investigation!" the girl said, vehemently. "This whole thing is as strange as—as that monster!"

Doc Savage's investigation was interesting. First, he visited his car, and returned with a small metal case on which were some knobs which were like those on ordinary radio sets.

"A device which howls when any metal is brought near it," the bronze man explained.

Doc now moved the contrivance about the room, keeping near the walls. It howled. He located a spot in the wall where it howled very loudly.

The wall, of wood paneling, looked solid at that point; but after the bronze man had worked on it a bit, a secret door came open. This revealed a safe door.

"Know the combination?" the bronze man asked.

"I didn't even know the safe was there!" the girl exclaimed.

Doc then opened the safe door.

HAD the bronze man unexpectedly moved a wall with a hand wave, the old butler's eyes would not have come nearer jumping out of their receptacles. He emitted a great croak of astonishment.

But Doc Savage was already taking a bundle out of the safe. There seemed to be nothing else in the safe. The bundle was letters, some new and some old.

Riffling them like cards, the bronze man inspected the dates. The most ancient was about ten years old, the newest only a few weeks. All were addressed to Leander L. Quietman.

Not a letter bore a return address.

Doc started to pluck out the contents of a missive.

"Your permission?" he asked the girl.

"You have it."

Doc spread the letter out. It read:

I am killing myself to-night. I hope that will satisfy you!

There was no signature.

The second letter read:

Hitherto I have been the exemplification of skepticism about things after this life. Perhaps atheism was my failing, perhaps only a lack of contemplation. But I have changed, and now I know there is a hell, and that it is expressly for the likes of you!

That one was not signed either.
The next one threatened:

I have made up my mind. I shall kill you!

No signature.
The fourth:

For heaven's sake, will you relent? I am ruined, but you continue to wreak your horrible work upon my family and relatives. Surely the human race cannot claim you as a member!
I do not know what I shall do!

THOMAS CANWELDON.

Doc Savage put the missive down, and said, "This is dated a year ago last January third. The day after that, a Thomas Canweldon went mad and murdered his wife and family."

Nancy Quietman had become pale. Now she sank on a chair.

"What does it mean?" she asked hoarsely.

Doc Savage did not speak.

The girl choked, "But grandfather—he—every one knows he is one of the sweetest old souls who ever lived. He has given millions to charity!"

THE girl, still seated on the chair, passed a shapely hand over her brow several times. Then she fell to looking at the bronze man steadily.

"I'm beginning to wonder," Nancy Quietman said slowly. "You started looking around in this room as if you were searching for something very definite. It appeared almost as if you really knew there was a safe here. Did you?"

"Not exactly," the bronze man said. "It merely seemed possible there might be a private safe here."

"Did you expect to find—what you found?"

"The letters?" The bronze man was silent a moment. "What I sought was proof of a theory."

"And are those letters the proof?"

"They are. All that is necessary for my own purpose, at least."

Nancy Quietman suddenly made fists out of her hands. She got to her feet, looking determined.

"Look here!" she snapped. "You know more about this than you are telling me. I demand to know the whole story!"

The bronze man relented to the extent of saying, "This affair is part of something infinitely greater than you imagine. It is, according to the evidence these letters contain, part of a mystery we have been trying to solve for weeks."

"I don't understand. What mystery have you been trying to solve for weeks?"

Doc Savage produced, from an inside coat pocket, a sheaf of newspaper clippings held together with a rubber band. He removed the elastic and handed them to the girl for inspection.

She read the first: It was the oldest. Exactly one year old!

NORFOLK STILL MISSING!

Police to-day stated that Elvin O. Norfolk, the financier who was reported missing by his family five days ago, has not been located. It was also stated that Norfolk had no financial troubles. He is a millionaire. His family furnished police with names of persons whose enmity Norfolk might have incurred in the course of business, and officials have decided none of these could have had a hand in Norfolk's disappearance.

The girl riffled through the others, catching only the headlines. The second:

UNABLE TO FIND BUSINESSMAN

The third:

ASSOCIATES REPORT JOHN COLE
"WINE KING," HAS DISAPPEARED

The fourth:

HUSBAND DESERTED, WIFE SAYS
COPS CAN'T FIND HUBBY

The fifth:

FOUL PLAY SUSPECTED IN
MISSING BROKER CASE

And so on. None were dated more than a year back.

Nancy Quietman, apparently stricken by a sudden thought, ran quickly through the whole sheaf of clippings, counting them.

"Twenty-two!" she gasped in horror.

"Exactly," the bronze man agreed.

"But grandfather muttered something about his being a twenty-third!" the girl cried.

"That," Doc said quietly, "puts your grandfather in with the mystery of the twenty-two missing men, which myself and my aids have been working upon for some weeks."

NANCY QUIETMAN was a young woman with courage. She took a gulp of coffee, which the bow-legged butler had thoughtfully brought while she was reading the clippings.

The bronze man drew another pair of clippings from his pocket.

"Just so you will be thoroughly puzzled," he said, and presented them.

The first clipping was from a New York newspaper, and bore a date sixteen months old. Just four months older than any of the others.

H. O. G. COOLINS'S MISSING
ASSOCIATES SEEK FINANCIER

It became known to-day that for almost two weeks private detectives have been vainly seeking H. O. G. Coolins, Wall Street financier and silk magnate. The detectives were employed by business associates of Coolins.

Police stated they have no clues to Coolins's whereabouts. Coolins's business associates refused to make a statement.

There was a column of that.

The second clipping:

COOLINS FOUND

H. O. G. Coolins, financier and silk magnate who has been reported missing for almost three months, reappeared in New York to-day.

Coolins only laughed when police questioned him, and asked the officers if they had ever heard of the Sea Angel.

Later, Coolins explained that he had been away on a private business trip.

He refused to explain what he meant by the Sea Angel.

Nancy Quietman shuddered violently and put the clippings down.

"The Sea Angel!" she said, after swallowing. "That man Coolins must know something about what it is. Why haven't you questioned him?"

Doc did not answer immediately.

"Coolins went about his business for some two months after he returned," the bronze man said finally. "Then he suddenly dropped from his usual haunts. He did not disappear. He just became very scarce."

Nancy Quietman nipped her lips. "You mean—he—perhaps he got scared of this Sea Angel—that impossible monster—and is hiding out?"

The bronze man did not answer, because there was an interruption. This came out of Doc's coat pocket, the rightside coat pocket, in the form of a tiny, metallic voice.

"Reporting, Doc," the voice in the pocket said.

Doc Savage immediately removed from the coat pocket a flat case which had rather well filled the pocket. He held the case close to his lips and spoke to it.

"You have something to report, Renny?" he asked.

The voice out of the case said, "Long Tom and I were watching the north side of the museum while you watched the other side, Doc, and we saw old Leander Quietman sneak away. We trailed him. He hurried home, got a bag, and took a taxicab to a steamship office, where he bought a ticket on a liner sailing for South America at noon.

"He gave a fake name when he bought the ticket. Then he went to the small office which he maintains in a building at the lower end of Wall Street. Probably he is in there now gathering up his papers, or whatever he would want to take along with him on his sudden trip to South America."

Nancy Quietman exclaimed, "A portable radio outfit!"

"What do you want us to do about this, Doc?" Renny asked.

"Where are you?" the bronze man queried.

"In the corridor of a Wall Street office building," Renny replied, via the tiny radio. "The steamer on which Leander Quietman booked a passage to South America is tied up to a pier not far from the foot of Wall Street."

"Seize Leander Quietman," Doc said. "It is possible he can answer some rather important questions. I am at his home. Bring him here."

"Holy cow!" Renny thumped. "He is as good as seized!"

Chapter IV

GRABBERS AND THE GRABBED

THE diminutive radio had hardly done justice to Renny's voice. It was a remarkable voice with the tonal qualities of an angry bear in a large den. Renny's fists were also remarkable, each being a gigantic piece of bone and gristle.

Renny was Colonel John Renwick, noted throughout the world for his abilities as an engineer.

"Long Tom," Renny's companion, was a very feeble-looking fellow. The truth was that he had never been ill, and could whip nine out of any average ten men he would meet on a street. He was famous for the things he could do with electricity.

These two assistants to Doc Savage stood in a third-floor corridor of the office building which they had mentioned to Doc as being near Wall Street. Through an open window at the end of the corridor, traffic noises and the shouts of a newsboy reached them.

"Grand jury fails to indict Monk Mayfair!" the news vendor was howling. "Read about it! Extra! Law cannot punish Monk!"

Long Tom said soberly. "According to the tabloid newspapers, people are beginning to talk about lynching Monk."

Renny also nodded. "I heard that, too. Well, we'd better grab old Leander Quietman."

Leander Quietman had entered an office near the opposite end of the corridor. He had come straight to this office after making his telephone call.

Renny and Long Tom went to the door, put their ears against it and listened.

They heard nothing inside the office.

But they had not the slightest difficulty in hearing a man behind them say, "Two Sneaking Sams, eh?"

RENNY and Long Tom spun. Then they batted their eyes as

17

men somehow do when they unexpectedly find themselves looking into the muzzles of guns.

The man who had spoken was almost seven feet tall, stoop-shouldered, and very burly. He had hams on his shoulders and practically no neck. He looked like the kind of fellow who would be at home in a striped suit, a ball and chain attached to one ankle, and a rock-breaking sledge in his hands. But he was nattily attired, even to a gardenia in his lapel.

The automatic in his hand—a big military model—looked new. Several other men behind him held the same kind of guns.

"What are you doing here?" the stoop-shouldered man wanted to know.

"Have you got a good reason why we should answer your question?" asked Renny, who was easily enraged.

"I'll give you an answer!" the man said, and stepped forward, lifting his gun to strike Renny.

That was his mistake. Renny's pet boast was that he could smack the panel out of any wooden door with either fist. Renny hit the man.

The latter's arms went up wildly as he sought to keep his balance. His automatic hit the ceiling, caromed off the wall. Long Tom caught it like a first baseman picking up a fast ball.

Two men slammed into Long Tom, banging him against the wall. Both grabbed his hand which had caught the gun. A man came up behind and whipped Long Tom over the ears with the flat of his gun. The man made faces and grunted as he whipped.

Renny rumbled, waded to Long Tom's rescue. His big right hand got hold of an arm. He jerked. The arm got a bend in the wrong place. Men struck Renny, kicked at him.

One of the gang ran to the end of the corridor, yanked a huge brass fire extinguisher out of its clips, came back, and after two false starts, managed to bump Renny's head with it. Renny fell down. Every one, except those holding Long Tom, fell on Renny, and it was soon over.

Every one lay still, or stood still, for a while, recovering their breath.

"These are two of Doc Savage's crowd," a man puffed finally.

The tall, stoop-shouldered man picked his gardenia from the floor and replaced it in his lapel.

"This may turn out to be a tough break for somebody," he said.

THE huge, stooped man then went to the door, turned the knob and went in.

"Why are you looking so scared for, Quietman?" he demanded, loudly.

Old Leander Quietman, who had evidently been crouching terrified in the office, croaked, "What—what—why, you are H. O. G. Coolins!"

Coolins swore, yelled, "Don't use my name!"

"B-but why n-not?" Quietman gulped.

"Shut up and put your hands out!" Coolins ordered.

A moment later, the huge, stooped H. O. G. Coolins propelled Leander Quietman roughly out of the office.

Leander Quietman seemed dazed, and very puzzled.

"What do you w-want with me?" he stuttered.

"The Sea Angel is after you, isn't it?" Coolins countered.

"Y-yes!" Quietman choked. "T-that's why I was l-leaving the country!"

H. O. G. Coolins snorted grimly.

"It can't be done unless I help you," he said. "I was a prisoner, but escaped the Sea Angel. I swore I'd get even, and now's my chance!"

One of the men said, "Hadn't we better blow, boss?"

"Yes," Coolins said. "We'll go now."

"W-why are you t-taking me?" old Quietman gulped.

"I'm going to destroy the Sea Angel," Coolins said, grimly. "When I came back, I immediately got myself an organization. This is part of it that you see here. We're going to finish the Sea Angel."

"B-but——"

"The Sea Angel wants you," Coolins stated. "We're going to use *you* for bait."

The men now got ready to go. Doc Savage's two aides, Renny and Long Tom, who had taken all this in with silent astonishment, were bound and gagged.

"We'll take them out by the freight elevator," Coolins said. "It opens into an alley, and nobody will see us."

Throughout the affair, there had been a man stationed on the stairs below. Renny and Long Tom had not known this, but they realized it the instant the lookout came stumbling into the hallway.

The lookout had the expression of a man being eaten alive by something invisible.

"The Sea Angel!" he croaked. "On the stairs!"

No small boy caught in a watermelon patch ever got into action quicker than did H. O. G. Coolins when he heard those words.

"Quick!" he snarled.

Old Quietman, Renny and Long Tom were seized instantly, rushed down the corridor toward the freight elevator. This lift was situated at the end of the corridor opposite the stairs.

But that delay had been a bit too much. There was a scraping and shuffling sound, and the Sea Angel came up the stairs.

Guns began crashing in the corridor. The bullets must have hit the weird monster; they could hardly have missed at that distance.

But lead had no effect on the creature!

The wings waved a little, then flapped, and the black tentacles whipped out. Each trapped a man.

Renny and Long Tom had never before heard men screech quite like those two did.

The victims fell, writhed, made awful noises. Obviously, they had been rendered helpless by some eerie power in the feelers.

Coolins left the two victims. He got the rest of his men and the prisoners into the freight elevator, banged the doors shut, sank the cage.

The loud breathing of the men was audible in the comparative quiet as the cage sank. It was the sound of a pack of hounds which had just run out of a scent.

BIG-FISTED Renny suddenly began to laugh. Being gagged, he had to laugh mostly through his nose. But he managed to get a lot of mirth out.

Science had explained everything, barring a few germs they couldn't yet see with their compound microscopes. This Sea Angel, this monster, therefore, had to be some fellow dressed up in a trick outfit. That grown men should be scared out of their wits by such a thing was ridiculous.

Renny thought it was as funny as a barrel of monkeys.

The men had cars waiting at the freight-elevator entrance. The prisoners were dumped in, and the machines left with noisy haste. Renny still laughed.

H. O. G. Coolins slapped him.

"You remind me of the good laugh I had when I first saw the thing!" Coolins snarled. "I don't like to think about it! I thought it was a man in an outfit. You think the same thing, I'll bet. Well, it isn't!"

"Whuz-zuhuhuz-wenn?" Renny said, which was the nearest he could come to, "What is it then?" talking through his nose.

"I've seen it *fly!*" Coolins snarled. "I've seen it swim under water, fifty miles an hour or more!"

The man's eyes were glaring with earnestness. Looking at him, Renny suddenly decided he did not feel so much like laughing.

Coolins gritted, "It's a *monster!* Bullets don't hurt it much. I guess they're not heavy enough. It can't be gassed, so it must not breathe!"

He interrupted himself to snarl at the driver for more speed.

"But it's got a brain, and can *think!*" Coolins groaned. "It's more clever than any human being! I tell you, it's something the like of which the world has never before known."

The cars headed north along a waterfront street.

"Whatcha gonna do with Doc Savage's two pals?" a man asked from the front seat.

"We'll kill these two Doc Savage helpers as soon as we figure a way to dispose of the bodies," Coolins said.

Chapter V

THE NICE YOUNG MAN

IN the uptown home of elderly philanthropist Leander Quietman, Doc Savage was waiting for Renny and Long Tom to appear with the old gentleman.

Nancy Quietman, having asked Doc if he knew who the men were who had threatened her grandfather, and received in reply a bunch of words which did not really answer the question either way, had turned on her grandfather's radio.

She sat listening to an orchestra moan through the latest song about a cowboy and his dying horse, and studied the bronze man, obviously with approval.

Doc asked abruptly, "Do you know a young man with red hair and a pug nose?"

Nancy Quietman wondered fleetingly if this was some roundabout method the bronze man was using to learn if she was at present being monopolized by any one particular young man.

"No," she said, after pretending to think. "I don't know such a fellow."

"Then it's probably rather strange that he should be peering through the window," Doc said.

The bronze man was on his feet the next instant, reached the window, noted it had a steel frame and bulletproof glass, and threw it up.

A young man who had been doing a "Peeping Tom" at the window was legging it through the shrubbery. Doc whipped over the window sill and set out after him. The young man glanced back, seemed stunned at the way he was being overhauled. When Doc was close, the fellow began dodging like a rabbit with a dog blowing breath on his tail.

It did him no good. Neither did the first blows he tried. He squared off with some boxing skill, missed two hooks, and was suddenly grabbed by the bronze giant and carried ignominiously to the study.

The gardeners, who seemed to have been collected on the

22

other side of the house, came running. Nancy Quietman spoke sharply and sent them away.

Doc took the red-headed, pug-nosed young man into the study. The young fellow was tall, athletic, and apparently unable to comprehend how his captor was handling him so effectively.

"Just who are you, anyway?" Nancy Quietman asked.

"Nat Piper," said the man with freckles and red hair.

A thump jarred from the study door.

The bow-legged butler had fainted there.

NANCY QUIETMAN leaped to the butler's side, and began worrying over him. Doc advised her quietly that it was only a faint, and that the man would revive unaided. After that, Nancy Quietman glared at "Nat" Piper.

"Why did he faint when he heard your name?" she demanded.

Nat Piper opened his mouth and made his eyes big. "Surely you don't think that made him faint?"

"What are you doing here?" the girl countered.

Nat Piper, instead of answering, reached out tentatively with one hand and felt of Doc Savage's arm in three different places. Then he shook his head and whistled.

"They must be muscles, but they feel like bone," he said. "I begin to see how you handled me."

He looked Doc Savage over intently. "Say, there's something familiar about you!"

"That is Doc Savage," the girl said.

Nat Piper acted as if he had swallowed a bug for a moment.

"Doc Savage!" he exploded. "Why, you're—you're—no wonder I couldn't handle you! I've read about you! I guess the description of you made you look familiar."

"Why were you sneaking around here?" the girl repeated.

"I had a business appointment with Leander Quietman," Nat Piper replied.

Doc Savage put in his first question. "What was the nature of your business with Quietman?"

Nat Piper took time out to marvel at the bronze man before replying.

"Art," he said. "I'm a promising young painter whom nobody ever heard of. I showed Leander Quietman some of my work, and I think he is going to let me paint his portrait."

Doc Savage made no reply. Instead, the bronze man got up and took a turn around the library. He paused to close the bulletproof window, which was still open, and while he stood there, he made for an instant a tiny, mellow and remarkably eerie, trilling note. This was a small habit which he had when mentally agitated.

Doc looked at Nancy Quietman.

"Do your gardeners change shifts in the middle of the morning?" he asked.

"Why, no!"

"A completely new set of gardeners has appeared on the grounds," the bronze man advised quietly.

The girl flew to the window.

"Oh!" she gasped.

The new gardeners had all started toward the house. Each man carried a gunny sack under his arm—gunny sack in every sense of the word, because it was obvious the sacks concealed guns.

NAT PIPER flung to the window, stared, rapped, "They're attacking the house!"

His voice was a squawk of alarm.

"I'll call the police!" Nancy Quietman cried.

She scooped up a dial telephone, listened, frowned, tried dialing, called, "Operator! Operator!" a few times.

"It's dead!" she gasped. "I can't get a dial tone!"

Doc Savage up to this point had shown no special excitement. He now dipped into a pocket and brought out a handkerchief, absently wiped his palms, then sat down.

Nat Piper rapped, "Aren't you going to put up a fight?"

The bronze man only looked mildly unconcerned.

Nat Piper snatched a poker and an andiron from the study fireplace, and charged out into the hall.

Following this, there was a great deal of noise in the hall-way, punctuated by such vocal emissions as, "Hold him!" "Damn!" and "Ouch!"

Then the raiders dragged Nat Piper into the study. They pointed guns at Doc and the girl, neither of whom moved.

The surprising development now came. The raiders seemed interested only in Nat Piper. They looked him over closely, even lifting his eyelids—they had knocked him out—to make sure his eyes were blue.

"This is the guy Coolins described!" a man growled.

"Yeah," said another, scowling at Nat Piper. "He's the guy we had orders to grab if he showed up around here."

Chapter VI

THE WALK-OUT

WHILE three men pointed guns at Doc Savage and looked as if they really wanted to shoot somebody, another man came over and searched the bronze giant. After a few explorative pats, the latter made goat noises of astonishment.

"This guy is a walkin' arsenal!" he said. "He's got some kind of a bullet-proof undershirt, and a vest with the pockets full of stuff! Who is he?"

"That's Doc Savage," some one said.

The man backed away, looking as if he had discovered himself smoking cigarettes in a dynamite factory.

"Does Coolins know Doc Savage is mixin' in this?" he croaked.

"Course he does!" snapped another. "Didn't you know Coolins just grabbed two of Doc Savage's men, Renny and Long Tom, when he grabbed old Leander Quietman?"

"What're we gonna do about 'em?"

"See if they're bulletproof," said the other.

At this point, Nat Piper tried to get up. He kicked a man's feet from under him, stuck a finger in another fellow's eye, then was knocked flat on his back. The shock when he hit the floor caused a picture to fall off a wall.

"Blast your souls!" Nat Piper yelled. "What're you picking on me for?"

"Brother," said a man, "we came here to get you."

"You've got the wrong man!"

"Coolins said a red-headed guy with a bull-pup face. That's sure you. Coolins said you would show up here looking for Quietman after that business at the museum. And sure enough, you showed."

Nat Piper looked at Doc Savage. "I absolutely can't understand what they're talking about," he said.

The man who had been searching Doc Savage, having gotten his courage back, now advanced cautiously.

"Watch 'im close!" he said hoarsely.

They watched, and if the bronze man had made a move, he would almost certainly have died. The man removed Doc's coat, and this uncovered the bronze man's vest. It was a remarkable vest, in that it was composed almost entirely of pockets.

The man began to look at the vest when he got it off. He then started removing gadgets from the pockets.

"I'll be damned!" he remarked. "Here's little bombs and grenades. Here's a trick flashlight not much bigger than my fingers. It's got a spring generator instead of a battery. Here's a little hacksaw, a tool kit for picking locks." He held up a flat case, said, "I wonder what's in here?" and opened it.

He then said, *"Hh-h-h-h!"* and got down on his hands and knees. Two men beside him coughed, and fell over, their teamwork perfect.

A man pointed his gun at Doc Savage.

Doc fell over on the floor and lay motionless.

The man with the gun, instead of shooting, said vaguely, "It got him, too!" Then he collapsed.

It required no more than a minute for everyone in the room to go down. They breathed, but did not otherwise stir.

Doc Savage then got to his feet.

THE bronze man had been holding his breath, and he did not breathe now—until he was out in the corridor.

He made a quick search of the mansion. The bow-legged butler was apparently the only house servant on hand, and he was unconscious with the others.

Doc went out into the grounds, roamed through the thick shrubbery, and at the rear, where the ornamental bushes made a jungle, he found the gardeners.

The gardeners were all bound and gagged. Doc, having inspected them, did not turn them loose. They would be all right where they were, and would not upset any plans.

The bronze man's next move was to drag all the senseless raiders to an upstairs room. He found tape in a bathroom, and gagged them. A drawer in the kitchen yielded enough clothesline to tie them.

Doc left Nat Piper and the bowlegged butler together. He did not tie either one. He did, however, search Nat Piper, but found nothing.

Doc rigged a tiny microphone—it was in one of the pockets of his vest—behind a picture in the room. Two wires which he attached to this were scarcely larger than human hair. He ran them to an adjacent room, and attached them to two binding posts, there for that purpose, inside his tiny radio set. The radio took care of the amplification from the mike.

Doc carried the girl into the room where he had rigged his receiving station.

Nancy Quietman awakened before long. Her first actions somehow seemed perfectly natural. She gave her hair a pat or two.

"Gas!" she said.

The bronze man nodded.

"But how did you know they would open the case?" she wanted to know.

"Every human being has curiosity," Doc replied quietly. "That case was not the only object in the vest which, if tinkered with, would release an odorless and colorless gas which produces quick unconsciousness."

Nancy Quietman looked at the bronze man and murmured, "I do wish you would tell me what all these incredible goings-on are about!"

Before the bronze man's silence had lasted long enough to prove he was not going to talk, the radio speaker began reproducing speech which the hidden microphone picked up.

Nat Piper or the bow-legged butler, or both, had regained their senses, because there was a brief struggle and a blow or two.

Then: "Begging pardon, sir, but what's the idea?"

That was the butler, of course.

Nat Piper said, "You know me! You know who I am, and you're the only man here who does! Savage doesn't know, and Coolins's men don't know."

"Turn me loose!" the butler croaked.

"Fat chance!" snorted Nat Piper. "I'm taking you with me. I can't have you talking. You won't get hurt if you behave."

The microphone was sensitive and picked up a rattle and squeak which was the window opening.

Doc Savage gave the girl her small gun.

"Those men, Coolins's gang, as they call themselves, are in a room upstairs," he said. "Watch them for me until I return."

"Right," the girl said instantly. "You are going to follow this Nat Piper and learn who he is and what he is up to."

Doc left the room silently, yet his silence somehow managed to convey to the girl that she had guessed correctly.

NAT PIPER scuttled away from the house by way of the thickest brush. He had tied a curtain cord around the old butler's neck with a slipknot, and held tightly to the other end of the cord.

Nat Piper took his prisoner downtown in a rattletrap coupé, the exhaust of which smoked. Doc Savage did not have much difficulty following in his subdued roadster.

The lower end of Manhattan Island is split down the middle by the street called Broadway. On the east side of Broadway is Wall Street, the financial district, with the world's finest collection of skyscrapers. On the other side of Broadway is a wholesale district with some of the world's worst buildings.

Nat Piper turned in on the wrong side of Broadway, and drove his car in to the curb between a moving van and a junk truck.

"Out!" he told the butler. "And walk fast so nobody will notice your goofy clothes!"

This referred to the livery the butler wore. He scampered, and they entered a door and tramped up stairs which squeaked like mice. The two climbed four flights of stairs, met nobody, passed no offices which seemed to be occupied, and stopped before a door which did not look as if it would stand much slamming. The frosted, glass panel bore a legend:

THE FINANCIAL ORBIT
Percy P. Smalling, Editor

A harsh muttering was coming from behind this door. When Nat Piper went in, the muttering became a man saying, "Let's kill him! Let's get it over with and kill him!"

"Let's cut his legs off first!" said another man.

"Hell, no, let's pull his eyes out!"

Nat Piper went in and frowned at several men seated around what seemed to be the reception room of the financial publication offices. They were the men who had tried to seize old Leander Quietman by playing at being wax Indians in the museum.

Boscoe seemed to be the individual whose demise they were discussing.

"Hello, chief," Boscoe said, looking at Nat Piper.

Chapter VII

SCHEMERS

THE other men all said, " 'Lo, chief," or "Howdy, skipper."

Nat Piper said, "Hello, girls."

One of the men explained, "There's nothing else to do. We'll have to kill Boscoe."

Boscoe grinned sheepishly. "Chief, I honest to goodness can't help it. I've told these guys what the doctors tell me. It's a disease. It's something I can't help. I've took medicine and everything, but it didn't do anything. I got——"

"You got my gun!" one of the men said grimly. "I don't know how you got it, but you did. Snitched it!"

"I gave it back, didn't I?" Boscoe demanded.

"Suppose I had needed that gun?" the man demanded.

"Well, it was loaded with blanks, anyway," Boscoe said.

"Do you want to help us kill him, chief?" a man asked Nat Piper.

Nat Piper said, "Boscoe, you must exercise your will power. You have a subconscious complex which makes you steal everything you can get your hands on. You must overcome it. You must exert your strength of character——"

"Right there is the trouble," a man said. "He hasn't any."

Nat Piper, changing the subject, demanded, "Where is Percy?"

A man jerked a thumb at the inner offices. "In the stink box."

Nat Piper urged the bow-legged butler forward, ignoring a man who wanted to know, "Who's he? The guy who was born astraddle a barrel?" Passing down a narrow corridor, the floor of which creaked, Nat Piper reached a door which said:

PERCY P. SMALLING
Editorial Director

Nat Piper opened the door, then ducked his head involuntarily against a gust of faint blue smoke and some awful fumes.

29

He coughed a couple of times, then shoved his prisoner inside. The bow-legged butler also coughed.

"Hello—*kerchoo!*—Percy!" Nat Piper said.

Percy P. Smalling had a box and a small contraption in front of him. The box was filled with black tobacco which looked as strong as incense soaked in liquid tear gas. The contraption was a jigger for making cigarettes, and Percy Smalling was manufacturing cigarettes with it. He was also smoking one of his terrible products.

"Have one," he invited.

"Heaven forbid!" Nat Piper said. Then he shook the butler. "But we might use one of them to torture this fellow into talking."

Percy Smalling drew on his cigarette, blew out a cloud of smoke which would have killed flies, and asked, "Who's he?"

"Old Leander Quietman's butler."

"Where's Quietman?"

"Coolins got him."

"What the hell would Coolins want with Quietman?"

"Bait to catch the Sea Angel, maybe. And maybe he has the idea Quietman might help finance him. He might be right, at that."

Percy Smalling was a withered collection of hide and bones who looked fully old enough for a pension.

"Just what happened, Nat?"

"Coolins sent his men to grab me," Nat Piper said. "Coolins must have figured I would show up at Quietman's home in an effort to locate the old man."

"Coolins is smart enough to figure that, all right. He's a tough mug. He would murder his own mother."

Nat Piper said, "Doc Savage is mixing in this in a big way."

Percy Smalling groaned audibly. "How much does Savage know?"

"I don't think he knows you and I and Boscoe and the boys are working for the Sea Angel," Nat Piper said. "At the museum, the boys pulled the gag of running from the Sea Angel in order to fool Savage into thinking they were fighting it. They also tried it on Quietman, and might have convinced him they were helping him, if the bronze guy hadn't showed up. But you can't be sure about what a fellow like Savage knows or will do. Maybe he suspects we're working for the Sea Angel."

Doc Savage overheard that statement, but if he got any satisfaction from it, his metallic features did not show that fact.

The bronze man was on the roof, dangling his little microphone down beside the open window of Percy Smalling's office. He continued to listen.

He looked mildly astonished when he heard nothing more. It was not often that Doc's metallic features registered an emotion.

The man of bronze moved the suspending wire slightly, causing the microphone to come in contact with the wall. This made a loud noise in the speaker. The device was still in working order.

The bronze man hurriedly reeled up the mike, stowed it in a pocket with the tiny amplifier, and moved to the fire escape at the rear, via which he had gained the roof.

His actions during the next fifteen minutes were as cautious as they possibly could be. At the end of that time, Doc was inside Percy Smalling's suite of offices.

No one was there.

The birds had flown. Just how, there was nothing to show. But they might have taken the simple course, and merely walked out.

Doc began looking around, and soon discovered how his presence on the roof had been detected. The place was fitted with a marvelously modern burglar-alarm system. The roof, for instance, was of metal, and a capacity balance system was attached to this. If a man walked on the roof, a light would come on in the alarm panel in Percy Smalling's office.

Doc gave the offices a going over. Percy Smalling seemed to be his own office force in the publication of *The Financial Orbit*. It was obvious from the reports in his desk and filing cabinets that he maintained an organization of informers similar to those who supply newspaper gossip columnists. The check stubs indicated these informers got paid only when they turned in something of value.

A large green filing cabinet yielded the real dynamite.

THE green file was full of fat brown envelopes. On each of these was a name.

One drawer was marked: "Finished business."

There were twenty-two envelopes in this drawer. All were fat. All bore names.

The names were those of the twenty-two men who had vanished inexplicably.

Doc Savage went through the envelopes one after another.

They were filled with sheets of paper bearing typewriting and handwriting. Reports. Tips from Percy Smalling's informers. And such tips!

Every one of the twenty-two men had pulled one or more sharp business deals. Nothing outside the law. Just a legal fleecing which they had given some one. "Legal robbery" more aptly described the deals.

Doc went through the rest of the file, which was marked: "Unfinished Business."

Each brown envelope bore a name. Some were fat, some thin. They held records of the business dealings of most of the big financiers of the United States.

Far more than the majority of these financiers had been entirely honorable in their transactions. A number had sacrificed their personal fortunes in order that others might not lose. Each of these envelopes was marked with a small star.

Other financiers had pulled some legal grabs. These deals were carefully outlined in the reports. And the envelopes were decorated with a black check mark.

Occupying a prominent position was the envelope bearing the name: "Lieutenant Colonel Andrew Blodgett 'Monk' Mayfair."

Inside was a full report of the scandalous, but apparently legal, swindle which Monk Mayfair had worked on an unfortunate and respected lawyer named Brigadier General Theodore Marley "Ham" Brooks. The report showed that Monk Mayfair had obviously robbed Theodore Brooks, and had, moreover, indulged in callous gloating about it.

Having explored all the envelopes, Doc Savage closed the file.

Several copies of *The Financial Orbit* were lying about. "Percy Smalling, Editor," was on the contents page.

The financial journal was a very reserved sheet, almost too conservative. Doc Savage was familiar with the publication.

It was not the kind of sheet which would have any use for such stuff as the envelopes held. At least, it never published material like that.

Doc Savage walked to Percy Smalling's desk, which he had already searched.

On the desk lay a newspaper. A late edition. The darkly prominent headlines dealt with the grand jury's failure to indict Monk Mayfair for the financial flimflamming he had given Ham Brooks.

Doc looked at the paper; it lifted slightly as a breeze caught it. The bronze man spun. The breeze had come in through the opening door.

The eerie-looking bulk of the Sea Angel was gliding through the door.

THE bronze man said nothing. He whipped to one side, scooped up the table, which was heavy, and ran with it toward the incredible thing now rushing toward him. He flung the table. The monster dodged back. The table landed so that it fenced the creature in a corner.

The snakelike, black tentacles whipped forward, and the round knobs on the ends would have hit the bronze man, had he not dodged.

Doc glided backward, got two chairs, and rushed. He sparred expertly, and managed to get one of the chairs wrapped around a black feeler. He twisted, and tangled the hideous black arm with the chair.

An instant later, the man of bronze managed to tangle the second dark tentacle with the other chair. He held both arms clear, rushed, and jumped against the monster with both feet. It went down. They tangled in a furious fight. The silver hide of the thing was like leather, and slippery.

The spectral thing of silver-and-black had not made a sound.

Again and again, the bronze man's fists struck. The creature might have been iron under his knuckles. And his blows had no appreciable effect.

The monster floundered. A tentacle loosened from one chair, fell across the bronze man's neck.

Strength all but left him. He could not see. Instinct alone helped the man of bronze roll clear, throw off the feeler. On all fours, unable to gain his feet, he floundered away.

When he hit a wall, he got erect. At once, his hands touched a window. His eyes were working a little. He could see the impossible thing making for him.

With his elbows, Doc knocked the glass out of the window. He got through, cutting himself some, hung by his hands, and dropped—blindly, not knowing what was below.

The Sea Angel reached the open window, and with some difficulty, crowded part of its macabre upper portion out of the opening.

The thing was there for several seconds. Then it withdrew, and whisked silently out of the office via the door.

Chapter VIII

THE WARNED MAN

HAM BROOKS was a man with a thin waist, a high forehead and an orator's mouth. He was intelligent-looking, and rather handsome. The nurses at the Gotham Sanitarium liked him.

Ham was in the sanitarium because he was threatened by a nervous breakdown, brought on by worry over his financial plight, the newspapers had explained.

Whenever they could, the nurses talked to Ham. The place employed some extremely pretty nurses, and the nurses probably knew they were pretty, and that they might help take Ham's mind off his troubles.

Ham also had his pet ape, Chemistry, with him. This pet belonged to the ape family, although there was some doubt as to just what branch.

When a visitor appeared at the sanitarium to see Ham, he was conducted in immediately. Company, the doctors had explained, was good for a man in Ham's depressed mental state.

The visitor was a tall young gentleman with a pug nose and red hair. He looked as if he might be a very strong young man physically.

"My name is Nat Piper," he introduced himself to Ham.

Ham, who was lying on a bed, looked at him vacantly.

"The Brooklyn Dodgers won the Series," he said, somewhat vaguely. "Wasn't that strange?"

Nat Piper frowned at this declaration.

"Don't worry," he said. "You are going to have your money returned to you. Do you understand? Monk is going to make restitution, even if he does not know it yet."

Mention of the name Monk acted upon Ham very much as if a gun had been shot off under the bedcovers. He sat up straight, moaning, shaking.

34

"A devil!" he croaked. "There on the wall! He's green with little sharp horns and——"

Nat Piper backed away from the bed and found a nurse.

"Is he always this bad?" Nat Piper wanted to know.

"He seems to be getting worse, poor fellow," the nurse replied.

Nat Piper made a grim mouth. "Has he any money left at all?"

"Not a cent. He is a pauper."

Nat Piper said, "I'll take care of his hospital bill, and I can also supply a few dollars for spending money."

"That would be wonderful," the nurse said. "But why should you do that?"

"Maybe I've been through the same thing Ham is going through," Nat Piper said.

WHEN Nat Piper left the hospital, he wore a fiercely determined expression. He strode to a waiting car.

Boscoe, the fat fellow who couldn't help stealing things, was driving the car. And Percy Smallings, the financial journal publisher, was in the rear seat.

"Drive to Monk Mayfair's penthouse. Boscoe," Nat Piper said.

Monk Mayfair's penthouse was one of the flashiest in the city. It occupied the top of a skyscraper near Wall Street. Part of it was devoted to an enormous chemical laboratry, for Monk was a clever chemist, and had perfected a number of chemical discoveries which had brought him a considerable fortune. He had already been a rich man when he had perpetrated his cruel swindle on Ham.

Not the least interesting feature of the penthouse was a marble-and-silver wallowing place for Monk's unusual pet pig, named Habeas Corpus. This wallow was filled with perfumed mud, equipped with health-ray lamps and other devices.

Monk was only a little over five feet in height, and was almost as broad. He had long, thick arms which were very hairy. His face was an incredibly homely one, with a huge mouth which was twisted in a big grin as Monk surveyed Nat Piper.

"Whatcha want?" Monk asked.

"I have just been to see Ham Brooks," Nat Piper said.

Monk's grin got bigger. "That shyster!"

Nat Piper said, "You robbed Ham Brooks!"

"The heck I did!" Monk jeered. "I was inside the law!"

"Nevertheless, you robbed him," Nat Piper said. "Ham Brooks may not be the first man you have swindled, although I will admit you have covered the other acts cleverly. We found no evidence against you when we examined your record."

Monk shoved his homely face forward.

"Look here, what're you checkin' up on me for?" he demanded.

"Simple," Nat Piper said. "You are going to return to Ham Brooks every cent you fleeced him of."

Monk brayed a laugh.

"Furthermore," added Nat Piper, "you are going to present one million dollars of your personal fortune, over and above what you return to Ham, to charity. The million will be a gift to redeem yourself with society."

Monk scowled. "You think you're serious about that?"

"Don't worry. I'm serious enough."

Monk suddenly roared mirthfully. "You crazy fool, whoever and whatever you are! Get out of here!"

Nat Piper said, "We always warn our patients. We give them a chance to repent and make restitution."

"What kind of crazy talk is this?"

"It probably does sound mad," Nat Piper stated. "But maybe this will help change your mind."

NAT PIPER now produced a small note book, to the pages of which were pasted newspaper clippings. They dealt with the disappearance of the twenty-two wealthy men during the past year or so. It was identical with the assortment of clippings which Doc Savage had assembled.

"Huh!" Monk growled. "What's this?"

"I don't know whether these warnings do any good," Nat Piper said. "Each of those twenty-two men were warned, too, but they ignored it."

Monk yelled, "You mean *you* are responsible for these men vanishing?"

"Not I," corrected Nat Piper. "The Sea Angel."

"The *what?*"

"The Sea Angel. A fantastic being which has come out of the sea, a creature with supernatural powers, an angel of vengeance which strikes only at wrongdoers."

"Then the Sea Angel will have to take care of you," Nat Piper declared quietly.

With that, Nat Piper backed out and hurried down to the street. He got into the car with Boscoe and Percy Smalling, and they drove off.

"What about Doc Savage?" Boscoe wanted to know.

"I do not think Savage is making much progress," Nat Piper said.

Chapter IX

THE TRAP

DOC SAVAGE was making progress. At least, he had recovered consciousness and the ability to move.

He lay on the sidewalk of the street in front of Percy Smalling's office. A curious crowd surrounded him. Three men in white who had evidently arrived in an ambulance which was standing near, were dressing various cuts.

Two or three persons on the street had seen the incredible Sea Angel at the window from which Doc had fallen, or rather, flung himself.

Police had entered the building, searched it, but the monster must have departed already by the back way.

Came a stir in the throng. A man shoved through. He was taller than any man in the crowd, and he was also thinner than it seemed any man could be and still live. He was just a bunch of sticks inside his clothing. A monocle dangled from his lapel by a ribbon. He was not wearing it.

"I'll be superamalgamated!" the man exploded. "Doc! They telephoned me you had been killed!"

"Not quite, Johnny," the bronze man said.

"Johnny" was William Harper Littlejohn, the final member of Doc Savage's group of assistants, or associates. Johnny was a noted archaeologist and geologist. He was also a man who never spoke a small word when he had time to think of a big one.

"Come on," Doc said.

And they left the ambulance internes protesting that Doc should have a day or two of hospital rest, as well as a thorough X-raying for broken bones.

Doc Savage, having evaded the crowd of curious, paused to address the tall, bony Johnny.

"You know where Leander Quietman's town mansion is?" Doc asked.

Johnny nodded.

"Quietman's granddaughter is watching several bound and

38

gagged men," Doc explained. "You had better go there and relieve her of the job."

"What are you going to do, Doc?"

"Investigate a man named Coolins." the bronze man replied.

JOHNNY left Doc Savage and took a subway uptown. The subway was the fastest method of transportation. A little later, Johnny entered the grounds of Leander Quietman's mansion. He knocked on the front door.

"Who is it?" a feminine voice asked.

"A coadjuvant emissary," Johnny said.

The girl thought that over, then said, "I don't want any. Go away!"

Johnny reluctantly resorted to words a normal person could understand and explained that he was William Harper Littlejohn, associate of Doc Savage, who had come to help guard the prisoners, also to question them.

He was admitted. The young lady, Nancy Quietman, had a gun, but put it away after she surveyed Johnny.

"I think one of those men would talk," she said.

"A pragmatical eventuation," Johnny said. "Er—I mean, that would be a help."

The man who the girl thought might talk proved to be a fellow who did not look as if he had been getting enough sleep lately. There was water and fear in his eyes.

Johnny hauled him away from the others, slung him down on a divan. Then the gaunt archaeologist and geologist began rolling up his sleeves.

"W-what are you g-gonna do?" the man quavered.

"Ascertain the frangibility of your ossified tissular substratum," Johnny said.

"Huh?"

"In other words," Johnny explained, "I'm going to see just how easy your bones will break."

The man was even more impressed than Johnny had expected. Possibly the big words helped the effect. The fellow rolled his eyes.

"W-why you gonna do that?" he croaked.

"We want to find out what's behind all this," Johnny explained.

Another voice said, "I guess it's about time you got interested in something else!"

JOHNNY spun wildly, and his grim expectations were fulfilled.

Men with guns. Several of them. And more of them coming in.

H. O. G. Coolins appeared, very tall and stooped. He looked Johnny up and down, one extraordinarily tall man interested in another one.

Having played safe, remaining in the rear until his men made the raid, Coolins now took charge.

"Look around, boys," he directed.

They looked around, and found the prisoners and released them.

"I'm proud of you!" Coolins told them sarcastically.

The freed men examined their feet intently and said nothing.

Coolins gave the girl a big, snaggle-toothed grin. "Getting you is a break," he said. "Your old granddad has got the idea he does not want to help finance my fight against the Sea Angel. I think my having you might be an argument to convince him he should donate a little money to my cause."

"Extortion!" the girl hissed.

"Let's get out of here!" Coolins snapped impatiently, paying no attention. "First thing you know, Doc Savage will be showing up here."

"What if Savage goes to your office, Coolins?" a man asked.

"I've got men waiting in my offices for just that," Coolins said, grimly.

Chapter X

BODIES THAT BURN

H. O. G. Coolins and his men entered two large, closed cars which were waiting, parked innocently in front of the Leander Quietman mansion.

"Get us back in a hurry," Coolins told the drivers.

They took half an hour to arrive at their destination, up on a bank of the Hudson River. The spot was north of the city, and deserted. The cars had groaned and heaved over a weed-grown road for the last quarter mile.

Johnny, when he was hauled out of the car, peered about. There was a boat tied up to the steep bank. At first glance, it looked as large as a liner.

The prisoners were hauled toward the boat, propelled up a squeaking gangplank and aboard. Johnny knew what the boat was then.

An old Hudson River sidewheel steamer! A hooker so ancient that she was no longer serviceable, tied here to the bank to lie until some one made an offer for her as junk.

A man turned on a flashlight, and Johnny observd that the portholes, the doors, the metalwork, had already been stripped off the craft. There was junk on the decks and in the corridors.

"A perfect hide-out," H. O. G. Coolins chuckled. "I own the old pile of junk under another name."

The gang heaved Johnny and Nancy Quietman into a cabin. They looked around. Also in the room were Renny, Long Tom and old Leander Quietman.

They could not exchange comments, because they were gagged as well as bound.

Tall, stooped, evil-looking Coolins was gone for a few minutes. During the time, he evidently conferred with his men. He returned with his mind made up about what he was going to do next.

He pointed at Johnny, Long Tom and Renny.

"Bring 'em along," he said.

Doc's aids were taken into the depths of the sidewheeler, to

41

the engine room. The old boat had once been equipped with two boilers—she was steam-operated—but one of the boilers alone remained. The engines were also gone.

There was one boiler, and a steam pump. That was all.

"Get that boiler going," Coolins directed.

A man put a crumpled newspaper inside the boiler, added shavings he whittled off a pine board. He built up a mound of kindling scrap lumber.

"The caretaker fires up the boiler every other day to pump the ship," Coolins leered. "The smoke won't attract attention."

Then he singled out one of his men.

"You go ashore," he directed. "Telephone the men at my office to get away from there. We're going to lay low for a day or two, and figure out a trap for the Sea Angel, with old Quietman as bait. And anyway, I've got to persuade Quietman to furnish me with some financial backing. I think he'll do so to keep his granddaughter from getting hurt."

The man who was to telephone left the old ship, got into one of the cars, drove a mile or so, and telephoned H. O. G. Coolins's downtown office.

H. O. G. COOLINS's downtown office—which he had been careful not to visit for some weeks past, incidentally—was situated in a building which, except for height, pretty much resembled the Washington monument.

The telephone cables which supplied the building with wires entered underground, through a single large conduit.

Doc Savage had tapped those wires—or the particular one which ran to Coolins's office. It had not been difficult. He had brought the equipment.

From where he crouched, at the end of the corridor on which was located Coolins's office, he could watch the door.

Doc got all the conversation between the office and the man who was relaying Coolins's orders. It was short.

"Boss wants you to come to the hangout," the man said, and hung up.

Almost immediately, seven men came out of the office. They were drawing on coats and lighting cigarettes. They were not a collection a peaceful citizen would want to meet on a lonely street.

Doc Savage was in a little niche at the end of the hall. They did not see him. By moving fast, the bronze man got down to the lobby in time to see the men leaving via the front door.

Doc did not follow them immediately. There was a very good reason for that.

Two rather plain-looking young men, loitering in the office-building lobby, had exchanged small signals. Then they fell in behind Coolins's men.

Doc watched. It was obvious the two plain-looking men were trailing the others. Doc fell in behind the two groups, far enough back that they would not notice him.

The trail led northward through the city. Two sedans, an old roadster and a taxicab. Doc was in the cab. It was the best kind of conveyance for trailing purposes.

A strange thing happened as the cavalcade went north. An unexpected thing. Other cars began to join the procession. When the northern end of Manhattan Island was reached, fully a dozen automobiles were trailing Coolins's men.

Doc Savage worked with the dial of his tiny radio outfit, trying different wave lengths. Before long, he picked up a voice:

It was Nat Piper's voice, saying:

"Broadway and One Hundred Ninety-first Street, north-bound," the voice said. A moment later, "One Hundred Ninety-second Street, still northbound. . . . Don't crowd us, boys. I think they're leading us to Coolins."

After that, Doc Savage kept tuned in on the transmitter, which was obviously operating from one of the cars ahead. If they got suspicious about the taxi, and one of the cars was ordered to investigate, he wanted to know about it in advance.

But they did not get suspicious. Coolins's men arrived at the river bank. The pursuers, Nat Piper's men, poured out after them. Doc Savage brought up the rear.

There was smoke coming from the funnel of the old side-wheel steamer.

Nat Piper said over the radio. "Let's open the egg, boys!"

THEY proceeded to open it.

Nat Piper's cars were apparently armored. They sent the machines roaring to the side of the old steamer.

Coolins's men scampered aboard the ship, took shelter, and began shooting. The bullets clanked flat on the armored cars, or climbed off into the sky with violin noises.

Nat Piper's voice in the radio, said, "Stick in the cars, boys. They'll line up along the rail to pot-shot at us. Then we'll take 'em plenty!"

Boscoe's braying voice yelled from one of the machines, "What about using guns, boss?"

"Only as a last resort," Nat Piper replied over the radio.

Doc Savage had ordered the taxicab to stop in the brush some distance back. The driver, who apparently did not know Doc, but who had done the trailing for a ten-dollar bill which Doc had shoved him, was terrified.

Doc got out. The driver headed back for the city at full speed.

Doc Savage slid into the brush, and traveled fast. He reached the river a hundred yards above the old sidewheeler.

Out of his carry-all vest, the bronze man brought an unusual contrivance—a nose clip and a mouthpiece mechanism. He inserted two tiny cartridges of chemical into the mouthpiece mechanism. Then he donned the apparatus, eased silently into the river and sank beneath the surface.

The tiny diving "lung"—the nasal clip and mouthpiece would also serve as a gas mask—was good for almost thirty minutes beneath the surface. It did not take Doc ten to reach the sidewheeler.

He grasped the huge blades of the paddlewheel on the river side and climbed.

The noise covered the sound which Doc made as he reached over and yanked the boards off a square porthole from which the glass had long ago been salvaged.

The bronze man swung through the opening. He listened. There was only the uproar on deck.

Doc went looking for the prisoners, not sure as yet that they were aboard. Not being a clairvoyant, he had not attached the real significance to the smoke coming from the funnel.

Chapter XI

DEVIL'S DERELICT

H. O. G. Coolins's voice rasped over the bedlam.

"Finish the job in the boiler room!" he yelled.

A submarine gun made a noise that might have been the laugh of an iron hyena.

"Four of you!" Coolins added. "Get back to the boiler room!"

A moment afterward, four men scuttled past the door of the cabin in which Doc Savage crouched. They did not look inside.

Doc, when they had gone, glided to the door. He did not seem interested in the four men, or what they had been ordered to do—the nature of the latter being something he had no way of knowing.

The bronze man listened, trying to locate the exact whereabouts of H. O. G. Coolins, instead of setting out after the four who had passed.

The four men were grim. They were not especially appalled at what they had been ordered to do. They were scared. Frightened by the attack from shore. H. O. G. Coolins, in his angry excitement, had neglected to tell them the attackers were Nat Piper's gang, and not the police.

So the four pounded frantically for the boiler room.

"We gotta get the bodies burned!" one snarled.

The five prisoners were sprawled out, bound and gagged, before the fire box. Renny, Long Tom and Johnny. Nancy Quietman and her grandfather. And the sides of the huge fire box were red from the roaring blaze within.

The victims had already been stripped of belt buckles, pocket contents. Buttons had been cut off their clothing. Everything identifiable that would not burn had already gone overboard.

One man seized a long stoking iron. One hand over his face, shielding off the heat, he lunged at the moaning fire

45

box, pushing the white coals aside, making room for a human form.

He pointed at Renny.

"Him first!" he barked. "He's biggest. He'll take longest to burn."

"I'll bet them fists make a hot fire," another said, playing wise-cracking tough.

The third man pointed at Nancy Quietman and the old man.

"Them, too!" he barked.

"But Coolins wants to use the old man——"

"Hell with Coolins!" the man yelled. "We snatched 'em, didn't we? A snatch is a caper they burn you for! They give you the chair! So we get rid of the evidence. *All* of it!"

The fourth man, who had lost his nerve, moaned.

The men laid hold of Renny. He was big. It took all four of them to lift him.

So they were in a group when Doc Savage came through the door.

THE bronze man had lived as long as he had because he did not take a chance that he could avoid. He had delayed following the four, seeming more interested in the whereabouts of H. O. G. Coolins. He had wanted to make sure Coolins was not going to send more men below.

It was four against one in the boiler room—until Doc reached them. He struck twice. It was easy. The men did not even see him. The two carrying Renny's feet went down and out.

The other two—they carried Renny's head and shoulders—spun. One yelled, dived a hand for a gun. The other also yelled, and sprang backward. He hit the fire box where it was red. Yelled again. Threw up his arms, sailed forward, and crashed violently into the bronze man.

Attack by accident, but the best the man could have made. Doc went down, caught off balance.

The other man got his gun out. He aimed. Doc lashed a foot at his ankles, connected, and the man upset. The gun put a bullet in the ceiling.

When the crook fell, he was close to Nancy Quietman. She kicked him. Both high heels, against his temple. It did not faze him at all. But the man yelled, rolled over and pointed his gun at the girl's head—and was hit by the man who had collided with Doc. The two floundered. Doc came down on them and used his fists.

That part of it was over.

One of the senseless four had a sheath knife at his belt. Doc used that and cut loose the five prisoners. He plucked the tape off their lips.

Renny and Long Tom, who had been seized some hours previously, writhed about, struggling to get up. They couldn't.

"Holy cow!" Renny thumped, in agony. "I can't—stiff—dang Charley horse!"

Long Tom struggled with arms and legs as rigid as sticks.

Bony Johnny got erect, weaved a little, said, "Metabatics are inutile, but of indubitable potentiality."

When he could think of words like that to say that he might manage to navigate, he was not in bad shape.

Doc Savage said, "Renny, Long Tom, when you're able, take care of the girl and Quietman."

To Johnny, he said, "Come with me. We may be able to catch Coolins."

"If anybody needs getting, it's that guy!" Johnny said, earnestly, using small words.

They left Renny and Long Tom to recover from the distressing effects of being tied, and headed for the upper deck.

The old sidewheeler was a large one, and Doc and Johnny had three companionways to mount. They climbed two, and the bronze man's sensitive ears picked up something that interested him.

"Let's see what it is," he said.

JOHNNY had no idea what Doc meant until the bronze man led him into a stateroom and peered through the cracks of a boarded-over porthole.

A cabin cruiser, a lean, fast craft, was approaching the old sidewheeler.

"Harbor police!" Johnny exploded. "No! They're not flying the police flag. It must be some yachtsman coming over to see what the fuss is about."

On the deck of the cruiser stood several men. They were equipped with rifles and tin hats. Doc drew attention to them.

"Yachtsmen do not usually carry that kind of equipment," he reminded.

Since standing and looking at the approaching boat would net them nothing, Doc and Johnny worked up toward the deck. They climbed a companionway, came out on a deck. It was one of the enclosed lower decks. The cabin was between them and the fighting men. They worked toward the stern, intending to survey the situation.

The shooting on one side of the ship suddenly stopped. Men began shrieking.

Doc Savage started running. Nat Piper had pulled some kind of rabbit out of the hat, judging from the sounds.

He had.

Piper's cars were close to the sidewheeler. His men had rolled down the armor-plate glass windows, and had poked nozzles through the openings. These nozzles were attached to cans resembling large portable fire extinguishers.

A liquid the color of yellow paint was coming out of the nozzles, turning to vapor, and the breeze was sweeping the mist aboard the sidewheeler.

Johnny exploded, "Gas!" Then he added, "But Coolins's men have gas masks!"

They had, most of them. But it did not seem to make much difference.

Johnny knew something about modern types of gas.

"This stuff works on the skin!" he barked. "You don't have to breathe it!"

Then he looked pained and began to scratch his arms and neck.

"I'll be supermalgamated!" he exploded. "The stuff is back here already!"

On the river side, a siren whooped three times. It was the cabin cruiser.

H. O. G. Coolins reacted quickly.

"The boat!" he yelled. "We're licked! Get aboard it!"

Which explained that the cabin cruiser was a craft kept near by for emergencies. Probably it had been kept in sight somewhere.

The cabin cruiser was near the box. Coolins ran for it. His men followed. Those who could not run were helped by those who still could.

Men began getting out of Nat Piper's cars. They had donned rubberized fabric suits which covered them from head to foot. Up the gangplank they scampered, like beings from another universe.

Doc said, "It is time we got Renny, Long Tom and the other two."

It was past time. When the bronze man and Johnny tried to get below, their skin burned as if alcohol had been poured upon it, then lighted. The gas had penetrated inside the old sidewheeler.

The bronze man directed, "Wait here!" and tried it alone.

He could stand the pain, the awful agony. But there was more to the gas than that. It worked into the body, absorbed by the skin, and brought on an immediate and overpowering weakness.

The bronze man's sight blurred; his huge muscles lost the feeling of movement. He went down, not stumbling, not wanting to go down, but just sinking.

Doc hauled himself back to the deck, found Johnny sprawled out helpless, and managed to get them both tumbled over the side into the river.

In the course of the next three or four minutes, Doc Savage came nearer death, probably, than at any other time in his strange career. The garments he wore, the mail armor and the vest, were heavy, and he lacked the strength to swim. Almost.

Doc Savage passed out completely, and came out of it to find himself on the surface, swimming feebly.

Johnny was in the water, a few yards distant. Floating, which was an almost supernatural feat, considering that he had almost nothing on his bones to make him float.

Together, they gained the overhanging bushes along the shore.

There was enough excitement on the old sidewheeler that no one had noticed them.

H. O. G. Coolins and most of his men had gotten aboard the cabin cruiser. The boat left—in much haste.

Nat Piper's gas-suited men raced around on the sidewheeler's decks, waving their arms and probably cursing inside their suits.

Shortly afterward, they began carrying the prisoners off the sidewheeler. Those of H. O. G. Coolins's men who had been left aboard had been likewise treated.

They loaded the captives into the car.

Doc Savage grasped bushes with his hands, hauled, strained. He was still lying in the water, but he was trying to get out, endeavoring to do something to prevent his men being carried off by their new captors.

Johnny croaked. "We've got—stop—that." He tried to get out of the water.

Neither of them had strength enough to make any progress worth mentioning.

Nat Piper drove away with his prisoners.

He was jubilant.

"Coolins got away, but we put a crimp in him," he chortled.

He had not seen Doc Savage, did not know the bronze man had been aboard.

"When the Sea Angel gets Monk Mayfair, we'll have this business nicely lined up," Nat Piper said.

Chapter XII

THE SCHEME

MONK, otherwise known as Lieutenant Colonel Andrew Blodgett Mayfair, was a fellow who had always claimed that he didn't care anything about his clothing. This was not the truth. Monk secretly admired flashy clothes. He had just blown himself to an outfit that was hard on the eyes.

Monk stood in front of one of the many mirrors in his penthouse, admiring the effect. Cutaway coat, striped pants, fawn vest, patent leather shoes and gray bowler. He grinned at himself, pleased.

Monk's pet pig, Habeas Corpus, wore a platinum collar which was studded with some rather expensive jewels. The pig was trying to push the collar off, using both rear feet.

"Cut that, Habeas, or I'll tie knots in your legs!" Monk ordered.

Having satisfied himself with his sartorial rig, Monk picked up a small brass-bound leather bag which had a metal mesh lining which could not be cut by any ordinary knife. In addition to the handle, there was a leather-covered alloy steel chain attached to the bag, and the end of this was fitted with a locking ring, like one bracelet of a handcuff, which could be locked about the wrist.

Monk opened the bag and took out an object wrapped in velvet. Removing the velvet, he admired the object. It was worthy of admiration.

It was a royal crown—gold and platinum, jewel-encrusted. A rich-looking piece.

Monk opened the newspaper. Inside was an item:

MONK MAYFAIR BUYS ROYAL CROWN.
PAYS MILLION FOR JEWELED PIECE

"Monk" Mayfair, the financial tightrope walker whom the grand jury failed to indict for relieving Theodore Marley "Ham" Brooks of a tidy fortune, to-day blew part of his swag. He announced that he had purchased the crown of King Emanuel Alfredo, one-time monarch of Spain.

The purchase price was slightly over one million dollars.

The latter part of the item described Monk's daily habits, stated that he was carrying the crown about with him so as to be able to admire it frequently. There was the added note that the police had refused curtly to furnish him special body-guards.

The whole article amounted to a subtle invitation to any thief who cared for the job to attempt to relieve Monk of the crown.

Monk replaced the crown in the bag, tossed the newspaper on a modernistic table, whistled at his pet pig, and strode out jauntily to ring for the elevator. But he did not ring.

He stared at the end of the reception hall. His small eyes all but hung out.

He closed his eyes tightly, rubbed them, then opened them again. The apparition was still there. He looked down at his pet pig.

"Sic 'im, Habeas!" he requested.

Habeas, the pig, emitted a dubious grunt or two and began to back away on stiff legs.

Monk squinted at the vision at the end of the reception room.

"I can't say I care for your looks," he said.

THE Sea Angel said nothing. It did not even move. Huge, incredibly hideous in the dimness of the reception room, it stood.

Monk, who had no nerves, grinned amiably.

"This is the twentieth century, the age of progress," Monk said. "You couldn't even scare a modern kid with that rig."

The Sea Angel remained motionless and silent.

"You ain't foolin' me," Monk stated. "You're a man, and you're wearin' a masquerade."

There was a stir behind Monk. The homely chemist spun. Two men had appeared through the doorway that opened on the stairs.

Boscoe, the fat habitual thief, and wizened Percy Smalling. The latter was smoking one of his awful cigarettes.

Monk jerked a thumb at the Sea Angel. "If this thing is your pet, you two guys had better get it out of here. I don't like its looks."

"That is the Sea Angel," Percy Smalling said.

"I told you about it, or, rather, Nat Piper did," Boscoe added.

"It," Monk said, "is a man with an outfit on."

"Hah!" Boscoe snorted. "What an education you are in for."

Percy Smalling looked at Monk and shook his head solemnly.

"It is natural that you should refuse to believe it is real," he said. "They never do think so—at first. But let me assure you that the Sea Angel is very real, and is, furthermore, a creature with powers which you might consider supernatural.

Monk yelled, "You two guys are the craziest-talking pair of loons I ever heard! Clear out of here! Get me? Beat it!" And with that, Monk flashed a pistol.

Things happened very rapidly. Percy Smalling and Boscoe put up their hands. That was only a stall. It kept Monk occupied. The next instant, one of the Sea Angel's weird, black tentacles had lashed forward. It wrapped around Monk's neck. The second tentacle got Monk's ankles.

And it was as if hot lead had been poured into the hollow parts of Monk's bones.

The homely chemist collapsed, helpless. Boscoe and Percy Smalling sprang forward, whipped out blackjacks and tested his skull for hardness.

"That oughta hold him for a while," Boscoe grinned.

Boscoe then opened the bag which was about Monk's wrist. He found the key in the chemist's pockets.

"Jumping paupers!" Boscoe exploded when he got a look at the crown.

Percy Smalling smiled widely. "It looks as if we have already got back part of the money he swindled away from poor Theodore Brooks."

The Sea Angel withdrew a few feet, shuffling. The thing did not make a sound.

"Let's get him downstairs," Percy Smalling said.

"Wait a minute," Boscoe protested.

Boscoe ambled through the other portions of the penthouse. As he moved along, things got into his pockets. Boscoe's acquisitive urges seemed to be those of a raccoon. Anything flashy attracted him.

And when he rejoined impatient Percy Smalling, Boscoe carried a sack containing something that kicked and squealed.

"What's that?" Smalling wanted to know.

"A funny-looking pig," Boscoe explained.

"Throw it away, darn you!" Percy Smalling snapped.

"But there's a platinum-and-jewel collar on the hog," Boscoe explained. "I couldn't undo the lock without the hog eating an arm off. So I sacked him and brought him along."

They picked Monk up bodily, carried him to the elevator and descended.

The Sea Angel had not stirred.

One of Nat Piper's sedans was parked on the street, a man at the wheel. The latter was not Nat Piper.

Monk was loaded into the car hurriedly. The men waited, looking around alertly.

"Nobody saw us," Boscoe said. "We might as well set sail."

"Wait," Percy Smalling grunted. "This fellow will come out of it before long. And I want him to see what happens up there."

The pig, Habeas Corpus, grunted and went around and around, sack and all, as they waited.

"I don't think he'll make good bacon," Boscoe said. "Too much rind to him."

Monk blew out several vast groans and opened his eyes. Boscoe stuck a blackjack wrapped in a handkerchief in his mouth.

"You yell and we'll pop you," Boscoe advised.

Percy Smalling said, "Look out of the car at the top of your skyscraper."

MONK, curious to know what they were pulling on him, looked out. What he saw made his eyes pop a little.

It was more than fifty stories up to his penthouse, and he had to crook his neck at a sharp angle in order to see. But there was no mistaking what he saw.

Up from the penthouse flew the Sea Angel. It could *fly!* There was almost uncanny ease to its movement. Like a stingaree going through water, it moved. Swaying a little, it crossed the street and was lost to sight above the other skyscrapers.

"All right," Percy Smalling said. "I guess now you still think it is a man in a trick outfit."

Monk did not say anything.

The car got into motion and lost itself in the traffic.

"Another three or four hours will see us where Doc Savage or H. O. G. Coolins won't be able to bother us," Boscoe chuckled, as the car headed toward Long Island.

Chapter XIII

ISLAND TRAIL

BOSCOE of the sticking fingers would have been affected painfully, no doubt, had he been in a position to listen in on what Doc Savage was saying about this time. The bronze man and gaunt Johnny were arriving at the hospital in which Ham, the swindle victim, was confined.

Doc and Johnny went quickly to Ham's room. Ham gave them a listless look while a nurse stood by solicitously.

"You only have a few moments," the nurse told Doc and Johnny. "He seems to be getting worse. Newspapermen were just here. Poor Ham was very bad while they were present."

Ham registered glassy-eyed approaching idiocy.

Doc Savage was carrying a small case. He indicated it.

"This is a radio receiver tuned to a transmitter in Monk's penthouse laboratory," the bronze man explained quietly. "In various spots around Monk's laboratory are switches, secretly located, which put the transmitter in operation so that it will send out a steady buzzing. Monk was to throw one of these switches if any one came to seize him."

The bronze man now turned on the portable radio receiver he was carrying. Immediately, a steady buzzing came out of it.

Big-worded Johnny said with small words, "Some one has captured Monk."

Ham sprang out of his hospital bed.

"It's worked!" he yelled. "It's worked!"

"Mister Brooks, please be calm!" the nurse said anxiously.

"Good old Monk!" Ham howled. "He put it over!"

Ham seized Johnny's bony hands and danced around the room emitting war whoops.

"Gentlemen!" the nurse cried angrily. "You are exciting him needlessly!"

Ham, still howling delightedly, skipped over and gave the nurse a resounding kiss, causing that flustered individual to collapse in the handiest chair.

"Come on," Doc said.

Ham, Johnny and the bronze giant sped out of the hospital. One of Doc's cars was waiting outside. In this machine, they headed downtown. Ham had brought along his pet ape, Chemistry.

Ham remembered how shocked the hospital attendants had looked and burst into renewed laughter.

"They didn't dream I have been faking," he chuckled. "And those newspaper reporters! They'll roast me alive when they find out that the whole swindle was a frame-up between Monk and myself!"

Johnny said, "The consummation was eminently paradisiacal."

"Of course the results are swell," Ham agreed. "It was a great idea of Doc's. We found out men were disappearing mysteriously. We failed to dig up any trace of where they had gone, or why. But Doc knew something was wrong, and became very interested because such mysterious goings-on are the kind of things he makes his business."

Ham paused to take a deep breath. "We could only find one thing in common about the men who were disappearing: They were all financial sharpers. Each vanished man had sometime in the past given some one a legal skinning."

Ham chuckled. "So we staged this thing. Monk gave me a financial trimming, by arrangement. He fleeced me out of all my money."

At this point, Ham looked suddenly belligerent. "Monk couldn't have done it without my consent! That homely missing link wouldn't stand a chance in a financial deal with me!"

When no one denied this, Ham continued.

"Well, the idea was to get Monk to vanish mysteriously, like the others," he said, "then trail him and find out what was going on. It seems to have worked."

"All but the trailing," Johnny said uneasily. "Better not get too confident."

THE bronze man and his two aids drove directly to Monk's penthouse. They found several persons still standing around in the street, gaping wonderingly at the sky. When asked, these individuals explained they had seen an incredible bird fly off through the skyscrapers.

"I'll be superamalgamated!" Johnny said.

They went up to Monk's establishment. It developed there

were hidden movie cameras in the penthouse which had taken pictures of the raid.

Johnny said, "I'll be superamalgamated!" again when they examined the films. From the cameras, the films ran into self-developing tanks which processed them immediately.

There was a good picture of the Sea Angel.

Ham, moved to incredulous astonishment, exclaimed, "It can't be real!"

Doc said nothing and went on the penthouse terrace.

After Boscoe and Percy Smalling had taken Monk away, the Sea Angel had walked out on the penthouse terrace. There were no cameras there, it happened, so there were no photographs of the monstrosity flying away.

"We have very little time to waste," Doc reminded.

All entered the car and drove northward, toward Doc Savage's river-front hangar.

Ham bought a newspaper when they paused for a traffic light. When he finished reading the editorial lambastings directed at Monk, Ham was weak from laughing.

"If they had only lynched him!" Ham chortled.

Any misfortune suffered by Monk always tickled Ham, providing it was a minor one. Monk and Ham had been good-natured enemies for years, and had never been known to exchange a civil word with each other.

This had made the present set-up ideal. Monk had gone through the motions of swindling Ham in order to attract whatever power was snatching swindlers and causing them to vanish. Nothing had seemed more natural than that Monk should finally settle Ham's hash for good. The two had been perpetrating petty insults and tricks on each other for years.

Doc Savage's river-front hangar outwardly resembled a warehouse. The sign, "Hidalgo Trading Company," on the front furthered that impression. The building was of brick, big and smoky-looking. The general impression was that it had not been used in twenty years.

Inside, it was a surprise. There were several amphibian planes, a speedy motor boat or two, a dirigible of small size and other conveyances.

The plane which Doc selected was an autogiro, a cabin type, not so fast, but capable of hovering. While Johnny and Ham warmed up the ship, Doc tinkered with a device.

The contrivance in which Doc was interested at first glance resembled an aërial camera which was mounted on a swivel and could be pointed at different places. But there was no place for plates. Instead, a headset of telephonic type plugged in.

Doc took this into the plane. The autogiro took off. Johnny flew, and, at Doc's suggestion, got two thousand feet of altitude.

After he had adjusted headset and knobs, Doc pointed his device at the city. He moved it about.

"I hope they took the crown to the same place they took Monk," Ham said uneasily.

No one said anything for a few minutes.

Then Ham grumbled again, "Inside that crown was a terribly small area in which to mount a micro-wave radio transmitter."

"East," Doc Savage said to Johnny, who was flying. "They seem to have taken Monk out on Long Island."

The two aids settled back and began to wear big grins. The device the bronze man was using was a direction finder of his own design. And it had spotted the diminutive micro-wave transmitter in Monk's recently purchased crown—or the fake imitation of that crown which the bronze man had supplied to Monk.

Two hours later, the autogiro was still in the air—well out toward the end of Long Island now. With binoculars, Doc and his two aids could see the car which was carrying the crown, and Monk, they hoped.

The cars—four machines, one behind the other—were traversing a marsh road. There were few houses. The Atlantic Ocean was to the south, Long Island Sound to the north.

"Look!" Ham rapped, shoving Chemistry off his lap to the floor.

The cars were turning off. They bumped over a road which was rough enough so that the gymnastics of the machines could be seen even from the air.

An ancient house perched near the Sound. Patches of shingles were missing from its roof. The cars pulled in and stopped.

The men, with their prisoner, Monk, unloaded.

Ham used binoculars.

"I see Boscoe and Nat Piper," he said. "But I don't see Percy Stalling. Hey! They're looking up at this plane!"

Doc directed Johnny, "We do not want to make them suspicious. Fly on toward the end of the island. Planes often take this route carrying fishermen out to Montauk Point."

Ham groaned, "But what about Monk?"

Which, considering the violent opinions he always expressed about Monk, was strange. Ham sounded concerned.

Doc said, "We will land at a spot where they cannot see us and return to investigate that place."

Johnny sent the plane on toward the end of Long Island, announcing that he thought it a good idea to get out of sight, then fly back with the motors muffled, and keep low so that they would not be discovered. It was a good idea.

Ham, settling back, muttered, "But where's Percy Smalling? We want to get him in the net, too."

Chapter XIV

COOLINS GETS A CLUE

PERCY SMALLING was already in a net.

He had just fallen into it. The net took the form of half a dozen vicious-looking men with guns. They had appeared as Percy Smalling entered the office of his financial publication.

"Behave, brother," one of the men advised.

Smalling was smoking one of his awful home-made cigarettes. It fell off his lower lip. He looked at the guns and became pale.

"Who—what——"

"Shut up!" they ordered, and searched him. They found no weapons.

"This is an outrage!" Percy Smalling declared.

"Matter of opinion," said a gunman. "You been pulling some outrages yourself."

"You must be mistaken," Smalling stated virtuously.

"You're the guy who gets the low-down on businessmen for the Sea Angel," the other reminded. "You dig the stuff up under the guise of getting news for your financial paper."

"Er—what kind of low-down?" Percy Smalling parried.

"You have been classing perfectly legitimate business deals as financial swindles and turning the information over to the Sea Angel," retorted the other. "And the Sea Angel then causes the businessmen to disappear."

"You have a quaint idea of what comprises a legitimate business deal!" Smalling snapped.

"We got some other quaint ideas, too. Get moving!"

The man took Percy Smalling downstairs and heaved him into the rear of a large truck, then got in and closed the van doors. The conveyance got into motion.

Percy Smalling looked steadily at a man who had been waiting in the van.

"Oh!" he said. "I begin to understand."

H. O. G. Coolins, the man who had waited in the van, smiled thinly and grimly.

"It took a lot of careful research to discover you were the one who gathered the Sea Angel's information," he snarled.

Percy Smalling, obviously frightened, removed one of his cigarettes from a pocket. They had allowed him to keep his smokes. He lighted it, blew out smoke, and some of the men immediately began coughing.

"What are you going to do with me?" Percy Smalling asked uneasily.

"You will soon know," Coolins replied dryly.

Smalling swallowed. "I'm afraid I don't understand."

"We're going to see what information we can get out of you," H. O. G. Coolins elaborated.

This did not cheer poor Percy Smalling perceptibly. He thought about it for a while, then attempted a desperate expedient. He tried to yell. But a wadded felt hat was quickly jammed into his mouth and he received an admonishing slap or two which made him see stars.

IN the course of time, the van stopped and Percy Smalling was tumbled out. He looked around. The van was inside some kind of large, ancient building.

A man yanked the hat out of Smalling's mouth.

"Have a good yell," the man invited, "and get it out of your system. Maybe it'll sell you the idea nobody can hear you here."

Percy Smalling, who could not see where it would do any harm, emitted a terrific bleat.

H. O. G. Coolins hitched up his trousers and produced a box of grocery-store matches.

"Want to make it easy on yourself?" he asked.

"What do you mean?" Percy Stalling gulped.

"Talk," Coolins directed. "We didn't grab you because we like your looks, or because we think you amount to anything in the Sea Angel's gang. What we want out of you is words."

"W-what kind?"

"Where can we get our hands on Nat Piper, Boscoe and the rest of them?"

Percy Smalling paused just a moment too long before he answered, "I'm sure I don't know."

He had lied, of course. H. O. G. Coolins knew it. He opened his box of matches.

"Strip him," he ordered. "And tie him across the truck hood."

They did this. H. O. G. Coolins began striking his matches

and sticking the heads into Percy Smalling's flesh while they still sizzled.

Percy Smalling screamed until his mouth ran red. After a while, he talked.

Percy explained, "They're waiting at an old farmhouse on Long Island." He described the location of the farmhouse. "They'll be there until after dark," he added.

"What're they waiting for?" Coolins demanded.

"The *Flying Dutchman*," Percy explained, moaning.

"Ah!" Coolins leered. "What about the Sea Angel?"

"I don't know where it is," the victim groaned. "You know that we ourselves never know where it is."

Coolins scowled, but believed this.

"We'll get Nat Piper, Boscoe and the *Flying Dutchman!*" he leered. "And we'll get the Sea Angel, too!"

His thoughts of what he was going to do made him very brave.

"If Doc Savage shows up, we'll fix him, too," he said.

Chapter XV

THE "FLYING DUTCHMAN"

By this time, Doc Savage was nearing the Long Island farmhouse with his two aids, Johnny and Ham. They had left the autogiro three miles back. Chemistry knuckled along at Ham's heels.

Woods were around them now and they were near the farmhouse. Wave sound from the beach reached them. Sea gulls sailed and squeaked overhead.

Birds were seeking roosting places in the trees, for it was nearly dark. There was a perceptible chill in the air.

Doc Savage said, his remarkable voice so low as to be almost inaudible, "Wait here a few moments."

The bronze man became a shadow in the growing twilight, and the shadow moved, and then there was no visible evidence of his presence.

The farmhouse had something the shape of a four-armed starfish, being two stories in the center, with one-story arms shooting out. Twenty years ago, perhaps, it had received its last coat of paint. Doc did not waste much time on the house.

Men were standing by the rear door. They peered impatiently at the setting sun.

"It's dark enough now," one said.

"Hold your horses," Boscoe rumbled.

"I've got the habit of holding everything while you are around," the man told him, and chuckled.

At that instant, a man came stamping out of the house and confronted Boscoe.

"That crown is gone!" he barked. "Boscoe, where is it?"

"Don't look at me," Boscoe muttered sheepishly.

"I'll not look at you!" gritted the man. "I'll knock your block off!"

"Aw-w-w," Boscoe muttered. "I guess I forgot and took it after all."

Boscoe now reëntered the house. Nat Piper and another

man followed him, looking angry and serious. They used flashlights.

Boscoe reluctantly lifted a loose floorboard, dug in the loose soil which was exposed. This soil looked as if it had been thrown up by burrowing rats. Boscoe brought out the crown, neatly wrapped in paper.

Sight of the gaudy bauble was too much for the man with Nat Piper. He swore, launched a swing at Boscoe. The ungainly Boscoe ducked, dropped both the crown and his flashlight.

The crown hit the floor and broke wide open.

Boscoe and the others popped their eyes at the crown. They could see now that the interior was not rich gold, but a complicated mechanism, electrical in nature.

"Radio!" Nat Piper gulped, after making an examination.

"Can't be," Boscoe growled. "Too small."

"It's one of those micro-wave outfits," Nat Piper explained. "They don't use much current."

He examined the mechanism further. Then Nat Piper reached a decision:

"Prize suckers we are!" he growled. "We bit on this one!"

He went over to Monk, and in his rage, gave the bound and gagged chemist, who reposed in an adjacent room, a kick in the ribs.

"You had that crown fixed up so some one could trace you by it!" Piper snarled.

Renny and Long Tom lay beside Monk. Near them reposed Nancy Quietman and her grandfather. All were securely bound and silenced.

Nat Piper, after another moment of thought, began issuing quiet, grim orders.

Doc Savage, watching the house, saw Nat Piper come out. He also heard what Nat Piper said.

"I think it's dark enough now that we can get moving," Nat Piper declared.

Men then came out of the house. They carried the prisoners. All of them.

"Half of you go down to the beach and see that everything is ready," Nat Piper directed.

Half of his men obeyed. It was completely dark by now.

Doc did not follow them because they did not take the prisoners. The men who remained behind stood around the rear door of the old house. They seemed uncommonly alert.

Doc Savage became very interested in this alertness. Once he made the strange, small, trilling sound which was his unconscious characteristic in moments of stress. It had a puzzled quality.

The men were waiting for something. Doc Savage was no mindreader, but he was a perceptive thinker, and in a few moments he realized that it had something to do with the men who had gone toward the beach.

Doc eased away, intent on investigating.

Yells, blows, whipping of brush stopped him. Then he traveled with the speed of a sprinter through the darkness. His two men! The fight sounds were from where he had left them.

A light came on. A very bright light. Doc used caution.

Nat Piper's beach expedition had circled and discovered Johnny and Ham. They had taken Doc's two aids, and were holding them to the ground. One man was lighting the scene with a gasoline lantern. Four others held revolvers. One had captured Chemistry.

The menace of the guns kept Doc from rushing in. The men were alert. The bronze man felt about for a rock with which to smash the lantern. But the vicinity was remarkably bare of rocks.

Before Doc found a stone, Nat Piper and more of his gang arrived from the house. All bore lights.

There was now too many of them to attack.

Ham and Johnny were carried, kicking and complaining, toward the old house. They were tied and deposited with the other prisoners. Doc kept in the background. As yet, Piper's gang did not know he was around.

Nat Piper looked at Ham and Johnny and scratched his head industriously.

"You're Doc Savage's men," he grumbled. "I don't get this at all. The only way you could have found us is by that radio micro-wave transmitter in the crown. But how come you are cooperating with Monk? Doc Savage threw Monk out of his organization for swindling Ham."

Piper rubbed his head some more.

Boscoe suggested, "Maybe this Ham was trying to find Monk to get revenge on him?"

"Maybe." Nat Piper snapped his fingers. "But maybe Doc Savage got Percy Smalling and made him tell where this place is!"

He dashed into the old house. There seemed to be a telephone line, because he could be heard using the instrument frantically. He came out wearing a long expression.

"Percy Smalling isn't at his office!" he snapped. "Something has happened to him. Doc Savage must have gotten him!"

Nat Piper had made a mistake. H. O. G. Coolins had seized Percy Smalling. Piper was aware of this error an instant later.

Some one in the near-by darkness put a bullet past his nose.

IT was a bad shot. The marksman undoubtedly intended to kill Nat Piper. Piper yelled, dodged.

"Douse the lights!" he squalled.

The lights went out.

"Get to the *Flying Dutchman!*" Nat Piper howled.

Doc Savage heard this. Naturally it was the first he had heard of anything called the *Flying Dutchman* being in the vicinity. The bronze man eased through the trees. It was almost entirely dark now.

The new arrivals were attacking. Doc had heard them coming, but there had not been time to do anything about it. The newcomers had rushed straight in to the attack.

The bronze man also knew who they were. Nat Piper had yelled out that something had happened to Percy Smalling. Doc had not bothered Smalling. Therefore, it must be H. O. G. Coolins.

Shots were banging wildly around the old farmhouse. Then men began coughing. Tear gas! Doc got a whiff of it, and retreated quickly. It was not the ordinary tear gas, but the kind which worked through the skin pores and rendered its victims temporarily helpless.

Nat Piper's men had evidently hurled the gas grenades to either side, leaving a lane through which they could reach the beach. They worked toward the water, carrying the prisoners.

Doc Savage headed toward the water himself. He had sampled the potency of Nat Piper's gas. He kept well back.

One of Nat Piper's men fired a Very pistol. The missile from this signal weapon burst into colored stars high above, skyrocket fashion.

From the sea came a replying rocket.

"The *Flying Dutchman!*" Boscoe yelled.

That changed Doc's entire plan. There were thirty or forty men embroiled in this murky affair. Whipping them was an operation that would require time. And there was a very good chance of getting shot.

A bronze ghost, Doc eased toward the water. The shore curved to make a small cove at this point. Instead of a beach, there was a marshy cut bank which sloped down sharply into deep water.

No boats were tied to this cut bank. There was a small, rickety wharf. But no boats. Doc had noted that from the air.

Reaching the water, Doc listened. Nat Piper's crowd was still coming. Coolins's men were still trying to head them off. Coolins's men were shooting steadily. No replying shots came from Nat Piper's crowd. But they were throwing gas grenades. When these burst, they sounded as if a paper sack full of water had been dropped.

Doc shed his coat, eased into the water. He sank and pinned the coat to the bottom with a small twig. He had picked the twig up enroute for this purpose. The coat would hamper his swimming. But now, if they searched the shore, they would not find it.

Boscoe and Nat Piper reached the shore. Boscoe made his hands into a funnel at his mouth.

"Get a move on!" he roared.

He directed this shout at the sea.

Doc listened, keeping close under the bank where they would not discover him. Not until he got his head under the surface did he hear oars. Water carries some sounds better than the air. Two or three boats, the bronze man judged. Approaching rapidly.

Doc sank again and swam out toward the mouth of the cove. He came to the surface. A moment later, the boats passed him. Three of them. When they reached the ramshackle wharf, Nat Piper's crew quickly loaded aboard with the prisoners. A man brought the ape, Chemistry.

"Get to the *Flying Dutchman* in a hurry," Nat Piper ordered.

Guns banged on shore. A flashlight spiked its beam at the boats. Boscoe fired a revolver. The light went out. Boscoe chuckled. Nat Piper threw a grenade. After it burst, there was not much shooting.

"Whoa!" Boscoe barked. "Maybe we can go back and grab that gang!"

"Too risky," Nat Piper ordered. "Keep going. We haven't got our gas suits. Anyway, too many of those fellows are still able to shoot."

The boats came on. Doc waited for them. Being interested exclusively in the shore, the men did not see him.

A few strokes put Doc directly in front of the first boat. He reached up, grasped the bow. Close to the water line at the bow was a ring, a heavy rope painter tied to it. Boats were often bridled thus to make them tow easier. Doc held to the ring.

Up to that instant, it had been the bronze man's plan to upset the boats. He would stand his best chance against such odds in the water.

But Doc did not try to upset the boat. It was a very pot-bellied boat, not easy to turn over. The bronze man clung to the bow ring. That way, they could not see him unless they leaned over the bow. And they were excited enough not to notice the extra drag on the boat.

They probably rowed two hundred yards. Then they approached something long and low lying in the water. This might have been a shiny whale. Waves washed almost completely over it fore and aft. No trace of light showed anywhere.

A submarine.

Doc released his grip, sank, and swam with power. He came up near the stern of the craft.

It was quite dark. The small boats were coming alongside the bow of the submersible. The occupants unloaded. Then the boats were yanked aboard and stowed away in large flush lockers.

DURING the excitement attendant on this operation, Doc Savage hauled himself aboard the submarine. A hatch aft of the conning tower was open. Nobody was near it. The conning tower shut off the view of those forward.

Doc eased down the hatch. He had a plan. It was to reach the engine room. From there, the behavior of the ship could be controlled.

Doc Savage was the product of an intensive training since childhood. He had studied submarines. He owned one himself, a small one which had been built for scientific investigations under the Arctic ice pack. He realized that this undersea boat was a German U-boat of World War vintage.

Once in control of the engine room, he would have the submarine at his mercy.

The man of bronze worked along an iron corridor toward the engine room. Then he heard voices. Approaching. Three men. Not yet ready to reveal his presence, Doc looked about for a hiding place.

A tiny steel cubicle seemed to be the only thing which was

offered. He stepped into it. The chamber was stacked high with boxes of canned food. There was barely room to close the door, once he was inside. He got it shut. Small ventilating slits perforated the top of the door, so there would be air.

Doc waited. The men tramped close.

Clank! went the hasp on the door. Doc was not often taken by surprise, but this got him flat-footed. He tried the door surreptitiously. It would not open.

One of the men outside said, "There's canned fruits and jellies in there. We won't need any of it for several days. Probably not until we reach the Sea Angel's home. But Boscoe will clean the place out if we leave it unlocked."

Another man chuckled. "Boscoe ate a whole case of peaches in two days on the last trip. You said it. We'd better lock this up, if we want any fruit."

A padlock went click and the men went away.

Doc Savage exerted all his terrific strength against the steel panel. But the human sinew which is stronger than steel, actually, has not yet been developed.

The bronze man made his small, trilling noise. It had a disgusted quality, for he knew he was not going to get out.

The engines started and the submarine moved.

H. O. G. Coolins, on shore, saw the submarine get into motion. He nestled a high-powered rifle to his cheek and pumped out cartridges until the magazine was empty. Throwing the gun down, he jumped up and down in a rage.

"We shouldn't have rushed them!" he snarled. "We should've sneaked up behind them!"

He swore at his men. Those who could stagger were stumbling about picking up those who could no longer navigate. The breeze had moved the gas cloud away. Some of them were not entirely senseless, and their moaning was impressive.

"How many dead?" H. O. G. Coolins gritted.

"Two," a man advised. "And I got a suspicion we shot them two accidentally. Seemed to me as if the Sea Angel's men were shooting over our heads."

"It's their boast they have never killed nobody!" Coolins snarled.

He got his gang together. They stumbled off to the cars in which they had come. The machines were parked some distance away.

They left the two dead men at the old farmhouse, first stripping all means of identification from their clothing.

"Maybe if the bodies are found there, it'll get Nat Piper into trouble," Coolins said, hopefully.

Percy Smalling was waiting at the cars, guarded by one man. Percy was a nervous wreck, trembling and mumbling under his breath.

Coolins looked at him and became more cheerful.

"He'll tell us the location of that place they call the home of the Sea Angel," he declared. "He may even tell us what route the submarine plans to take. If we can catch that undersea boat enroute, what we'll do to it will be plenty."

"Something like a nice depth bomb?" a man asked.

"Something like that," Coolins agreed. "Make it snappy. We have to get planes."

Chapter XVI

THE "PATIENT"

DIESEL engines were driving the submarine along the surface at a fair speed. Indicators in the control room showed the ballast tanks were almost fully blown, yet the craft rode low in the water. At times, waves gurgled entirely over her. Two lookouts in the conning tower wore oilskins and had a wet job.

Nat Piper and Boscoe gave a few orders about the course. The men were to keep the undersea boat out of waters frequented by boats. And at the slightest sign of any craft, they were to dive.

This done, Nat and Boscoe went below to a tiny steel cabin where the prisoners were confined. Orders were issued. Pretty Nancy Quietman, Ham, Johnny, Long Tom and Renny it seemed, were to be merely locked in a cabin. Two cabins, rather. The young woman was to have one by herself.

"It is unfortunate we had to bring you along," Nat Piper explained, grinning boyishly. "We regret it is much as you do. You will simply be prisoners, but well-treated captives if you behave. Perhaps what you see in the next few weeks will be a profound lesson to you."

He ignored their angry demands for an explanation of what was ahead of them.

"Take those two to the engine room," he ordered, pointing at Monk and old Leander L. Quietman, the noted philanthropist and lover of mankind.

These two were hauled into the engine room. The hauling was none too gentle.

Every spare inch of the submersible was occupied by stored goods. Food, largely. But lashed to pipes in an unused corner of the engine room were several remarkable-looking objects. Each of these consisted of a long and heavy metal yoke.

This was almost six feet long and looked like nothing so much as two heavy archers' bows with the ends bolted together. To each end was fastened a chain, and at the other end of the chains dangled ankle irons.

71

Monk did some indignant kicking, but before long he found his neck inside one of the bows. It was bolted, and the ends of the bows riveted over the taps. The ankle irons were fastened around Monk's ankles. Then he was untied and ungagged.

Monk immediately started a fight. He swung at a foe, but the latter dodged. Monk tried to rush Boscoe. The ankle irons jerked the yokes against his neck and he fell down heavily. He got up looking enraged and sheepish.

"Hey!" he complained. "I can't stand up straight with this rig on!"

"Just what we had hoped," Nat Piper smiled.

Poor old Leander L. Quietman was subjected to the same treatment.

This made Monk even more angry. Old Quietman looked so pitiful.

"A fine bunch of tramps!" Monk yelled. "Picking on an old man!"

Nat Piper said grimly, "If this old man got what he deserved, he would go to the electric chair!"

Monk and Leander L. Quietman were now locked in a tiny stateroom. Their prison looked small when they first entered, and seemed to get smaller the longer they were in it. They discovered that when one wanted to stand up and stretch, the other would have to stay in one of the two berths. There was an upper and lower berth, both painfully hard.

Elderly Leander Quietman moaned, "I cannot understand why they accuse me of being a bad man. For many years, I have given to charity and helped poor unfortunates. I thought every one knew I was a good man."

Monk had been puzzled about that, too.

THE submarine lumbered steadily ahead. In a few hours, it began rolling as only an undersea boat can roll.

Renny, Long Tom, Johnny and Ham, confined in one cabin, wore plain khaki coveralls. The only garments they had been permitted to retain. Their best efforts unearthed no way of escaping from the cell.

"Where are we?" they yelled at a passing man, whom they could see through the ventilating slits in their door.

"You're on the *Flying Dutchman*," the man advised. "There's no name on her, so I guess you didn't know. But that's what we call her."

"She's an old World War U-boat, isn't she?" asked Renny, whose engineering knowledge included a bit about submarines.

"Right," agreed the man. "You wouldn't think she laid under the sea for twenty years, would you?"

"Huh?"

"Her port diving rudders must have fouled a mine net which then tangled with the propellers," the man explained. "She could not get to the surface and her crew were overcome by lack of oxygen."

"Is this a straight story?" Renny demanded.

"Oh, it's true enough," the man said. "There was an item in the newspapers about a fisherman seeing her when she came to the surface. You see, the net which fouled her eventually rusted free of its anchor and the old tub still had enough air in her to rise. She's a remarkably tight craft."

Renny rumbled, "So that's how you got her?"

"Nat Piper happened to be close by," the man said. "He took charge of her, and——"

Nat Piper himself, who had come up, said, "I wouldn't talk too much."

The man said, "Yes, sir!" and left.

The prisoners tried to get Nat Piper to talk to them, but he walked away. After which the captives tried to make things disagreeable by shouting and yelling. They did it in relays, hoping to keep any one from sleeping. Renny's great voice was particularly good at this.

But their captors appeared with an iron plate which they fastened over the ventilating slits. Soon the air in the tiny cubicle ran out, and the prisoners were very glad to promise to keep quiet.

After that, the *chung-alung-chung-chung* of the Diesels got very monotonous indeed. The fact that the air was none too aromatic did not help. Its sustaining qualities seemed good enough, however.

It was sometime the next day when Monk and poor Leander Quietman were hauled out of their uncomfortable cubicle.

WHILE the two unlucky prisoners stood in hunched positions because of their yokes and chains, they were handed a pail of suds and two brushes.

"Scrub!" they were ordered. "And after you get done, the dishes will be ready to wash."

"Not me!" Monk roared, and threw his brush at the nearest tormenter, knocking that worthy temporarily unconscious. Monk then followed up by dousing fat Boscoe with the pail of suds.

Boscoe wiped his smarting eyes. "How about the water treatment, boss?"

"Go ahead," Nat Piper directed.

Monk and elderly Quietman were taken on deck. It was rather cold. They shivered. Ropes were tied to their yokes and they were flung overboard. It was really cold then. Furthermore, they were nearly drowned after being towed behind the submarine for a while.

They decided the scrubbing job was preferable.

"This yoke hurts my neck," Monk complained. "It's heavy!"

Nat Piper laughed cheerfully and said, "That yoke is the weight of your sins bearing down on you."

"Just what in blazes do you mean?" Monk gritted.

"Haven't you guessed what you are in for?" Nat Piper demanded.

"I got a suspicion. But suppose you tell me."

"The Sea Angel is reforming rich men who got their money at the expense of other people. You got yours that way. At least, you got part of it by swindling Ham Brooks. We are going to make you suffer for it. You are going to suffer until you decide you will never make another dollar wrongfully. You will suffer until you decide to give back what you have taken. Then, if your suffering properly reforms you, and you promise never to do a wrongful act again, we may give you another chance."

Monk scratched his head and eyed Nat Piper. He decided young Piper did not look like a bad egg, and his idea, if he was telling the truth, was not an unworthy one. But Monk did not care for the method.

Monk pointed at poor old Leander L. Quietman. "You're abusing this poor old fellow, Piper. Quietman is a philanthropist who is well known for his kindness."

Nat Piper looked at Leander L. Quietman with utter disgust.

"That old man is the most two-faced old reprobate who ever lived!" Piper gritted. "For years, he has pretended to be a fine old lover of mankind. And on the side, he has perpetrated business swindles. He has been utterly merciless. Not less than half a dozen suicides are chalked up against him. Men he has ruined."

Monk looked at white-haired old Quietman. "Anything to that?"

"It's a dirty lie!" Quietman snarled.

But the old man's face was twisted, and there was some-

thing in the shape of his snarl, the utter ferocity and despera-
tion in his eyes, that Monk had never noticed before.

Monk took a deep breath. It was as if he were seeing a
weasel in a coop of small chickens which it had slaughtered.
Monk suddenly knew that nice-looking Leander L. Quietman,
the old gentleman with the saintly reputation, was a wolf in a
sheep's garb.

"Whew!" Monk gulped. "Whew!"

Monk then decided it was time Nat Piper had the truth
about himself.

"Say, Piper," Monk asked tentatively, "if I wasn't really a
swindler, would I get different treatment?"

"Of course," Nat Piper said.

Monk sighed his relief. "Well, I'm not. I only faked that
trimming of Ham. The idea was to have me play the part of a
bait to find out what had been making wealthy business
sharpers vanish."

The reactions to this were not exactly what Monk had hoped
for. Nat Piper emitted a roar of laughter, and Boscoe echoed
it.

"You financial wolves are expert liars!" Nat Piper chuckled.
"You think of the dangedest stories to get yourselves out of
your troubles!"

"You don't believe me?" Monk exploded.

"Of course not!" Nat Piper snapped. "And for telling that
lie, you can wash a double share of the dirty dishes and polish
the boots of everybody aboard!"

Monk's groan was something calculated to melt the heart of
a snow man. Nor was his injured feeling softened when he
heard stifled laughter from the chamber where Ham was
confined. Ham, Monk realized, had overheard.

And any misfortune befalling Monk, as long as it did not
endanger the homely chemist's life, invariably tickled Ham.

THREE more days of travel in the submarine became very
monotonous. By that time, even the crew were barking at each
other occasionally.

Boscoe in particular was suffering. It was his own fault.
The homely, fat fellow who could not help stealing things
had been banished to a pallet on the floor of the torpedo room
forward.

Boscoe's mates had become tired of collecting their watches,
money, guns, belt buckles, even their shoes, from the places

where Boscoe hid them after he could not help stealing them.

Another thing was working on Boscoe. He loved fruit. If fresh fruit was not at hand, the canned variety would do. And he could not find the store of canned fruit which he knew should be aboard.

Accordingly, Boscoe was devoting his spare time to surreptitious prowling in search of the canned delicacies. He was methodical about it. He began at the bow and worked aft. He found a number of things which he fondled longingly, then put back, for the fruit was uppermost on his mind.

In the course of time, Boscoe located a lazaret which was padlocked. He reasoned the fruit was inside. So he repaired to the engine room and, while no one was observing, carefully fashioned himself a tool for picking locks. Boscoe had had some experience along these lines.

His tool worked remarkably well on the padlock, opening it with the first try. Boscoe peered up and down the narrow passage, made sure no one was in sight, then opened the door and reached in eagerly for a case of fruit.

What he got was a terrific wallop on the chin. It should have knocked him senseless, and did stun him. He fell limply, not making a sound. His small eyes ogled the giant bronze man who had struck him.

Only then did Boscoe realize he had discovered Doc Savage.

The unfortunate part of the incident was that Nat Piper and two other men also realized it—after they came unexpectedly into the passage. A man with Piper was one of the engineers. He had seen Boscoe make his tool and had guessed that they would have to look after their canned fruit supply.

Nat Piper yanked out a small Boy Scout whistle and blew a terrific blast.

Doc Savage rushed. Nat Piper put up his fists. He should have run, although Doc would probably have caught him. The bronze man had fared well on a juicy canned fruit diet. Piper felt something like an explosion on his chin. It was a while before he felt anything else.

The other two men ran. Doc pursued them. The two had a slight start. They skinned themselves while getting through a bulkhead door. They slammed the door, dogged it tight on the other side.

Doc spun. He knew he was in a water-tight compartment alone. It would be a good idea to get out of it.

He did not make it. Men drawn by the whistles came running from the other direction, saw him, banged the door in the other bulkhead before he could stop them. He was locked in a water-tight chamber, or section, of the submarine.

The rest was easy.

The compartments were equipped so they could be pumped separately. By the same token, water could be flushed in. The crew did this.

Before the water was up to his knees, Doc banged on the bulkhead and surrendered. There was nothing else he could do.

It was just as well he gave up when he did, because they made him pump the water out of the compartment by hand. It was no easy job.

Chapter XVII

THE GUARDIAN ANGEL

As soon as Doc Savage finished pumping, he was equipped with one of the yokes and leg-iron contrivances. They then conducted him to Nat Piper, who had revived and was examining his jaw with a hand mirror.

"You pack a wallop," Piper grinned.

Doc Savage said nothing.

Nat Piper studied the giant bronze man for a time. He was obviously impressed by the remarkable physique he was observing, because he whistled quietly.

"I've always admired you," he said, frankly. "You are more or less engaged in the same kind of work as my—my—er, the Sea Angel."

Doc did not seem particularly interested.

"You right wrongs and punish evildoers," Nat Piper said. "The Sea Angel is doing the same thing. Only in a more effective way."

Doc said, "A way that is not practical."

"I think it's as practical as hell!" Nat Piper laughed. "You should see our results."

"One of your graduates has been running around New York —running after you and me part of the time," Doc offered dryly.

Nat Piper looked uncomfortable.

"H. O. G. Coolins is the individual referred to," Doc said.

"I know who you're referring to!" Piper snapped.

"Coolins took your course of training, didn't he?"

"He was an exception," Nat Piper explained gloomily. "The others won't be like him."

"How do you know? Coolins is the only one you have graduated so far, is he not?"

"Yes," Piper admitted. "Say, you seem to know a lot about us."

"Only some guesswork," the bronze man explained.

78

"Well, it's good guesswork. We've been taking these rich financial gobblers and putting them through the mill. Boy, we really give them hell! And when we figure we've got them cured, we will turn them loose. They'll be changed men."

Doc Savage said nothing.

NAT PIPER seemed to consider, and reach a conclusion. The quickness with which he came to this conclusion was some slight proof that he had toyed with the idea previously.

"Look here," Piper said. "Maybe the Sea Angel will let you work with us in this. You'd be a lot of help to us. You'd be doing a good work for the world. How about it? Will you aid us if the Sea Angel will consent to the idea?"

"No," Doc said.

"Huh?"

"Not a chance."

"But why not, blast it? Your life's work is something along the same line."

"Your method," the bronze man said, "will never be successful."

"The heck it won't! We put the fear into them!"

Doc Savage explained patiently. "Your system is psychologically wrong. Criminal tendencies are the result of a maladjustment of certain little-known glands in the human body. Fear of punishment is only a temporary deterrent to a criminal. Submitting the individual of criminal tendencies to physical pain and hardships only aggravates the condition in most cases. The only feasible cure is an operation or nonsurgical treatment of the defective glands which are causing the individual to become non-social."

"I don't go for that scientific claptrap!" Nat Piper declared. "Scare hell out of them and they won't dare fleece anybody again."

"H. O. G. Coolins, for instance," Doc said.

"Aw, nuts!" Nat Piper snapped. "He was an exception. Oh, well, if you won't go in with us, you won't."

"Your scheme is admirable in purpose, but positively will not work in actual practice," Doc Savage said levelly. "If it were possible to cure crooks by the method you are using, I should be the first to offer my aid."

Nat Piper sighed. Then he put a sharp question.

"You don't think the Sea Angel is real, do you?" he demanded.

Doc Savage did not answer.

"It's real, all right," Nat Piper said. "I think you'll realize that before long."

JUST what Nat Piper meant was not evident until some twelve hours later, when Doc Savage was hauled from the small storeroom where he had been confined. The submarine was wallowing in a greasy sea.

It was very dark. A gasoline lantern was blazing on deck. This light disclosed a considerable gathering.

Pretty Nancy Quietman was there. She gazed at Doc and managed a small smile.

"This is an incredible predicament, isn't it?" she said quietly.

All the other prisoners were on deck.

Nat Piper cleared his throat noisily and said, "It occurred to me that all of you might like to see that the master of your destinies is still with you. Look!"

He pointed over the side.

They all looked. What they saw was unexpected and caused several to all but stop breathing.

The Sea Angel! It was swimming beside the submarine, about ten feet beneath the surface. Although it was night, the thing showed up distinctly. It was phosphorescent in nature. It glowed. It writhed and fluttered as it swam, darting about a bit. Even the long, fearsome cords attached to its queer wings glowed with an uncanny luminance. These cords were trailing behind the creature as it swam.

"Whew!" exploded homely Monk.

"Well, bless me!" echoed Ham. It was the first time Ham had seen the impossible thing.

Nat Piper allowed them all time for a good look, then gave orders.

"Get below," he directed. "The Sea Angel has been accompanying us since we left Long Island Sound. He—it prefers to travel by itself, rather than in the submarine. Sometimes it flies through the air."

"Somebody here is crazy!" Ham said, positively.

"Speak for yourself," Monk grumbled.

"That thing is some kind of trick!" Ham snapped. "It can't be real!"

"That," said Nat Piper, "is what I am trying to prove to you. It is real!"

The prisoners were herded below decks and returned to their respective places of confinement.

Once more, time dragged. But it was only five or six hours.

Then, it developed, the prisoners were to be permitted to dine together. The place where they messed was the combination crew's quarters and dining room forward. The food was plain but palatable, with two exceptions:

Monk and old Quietman were given nothing but bread and water.

"I ain't gonna put up with this!" Monk explained. "I've already lost twenty pounds!"

Old Leander L. Quietman glared malevolently. The old man seemed to have undergone a marked change. It was as if the philanthropist and man who did nice things for the poor was only a veneer, and hardship was wearing it off, showing the vicious old rascal beneath. The true reprobate that most of the world had never dreamed existed.

The prisoners were cautiously led aft, one at a time. They passed under an open hatch. And, of course, they glanced up. And each one saw the Sea Angel.

The fantastic thing was flying along, not more than fifty feet above the submarine! Its triangular, finlike wings moved lazily as it kept pace with the submarine.

It was foggy outside, but it was also daylight, and the monster was plainly visible.

The prisoners were silent, impressed, after they were returned to their posts.

An hour later, the submarine dived suddenly. It seemed that a ship had been sighted on the horizon.

"We don't want to take chances!" Nat Piper yelled. "We were seen twice before, but the reports were just passed off as a mistake. But we don't want it to happen too often!"

Chapter XVIII

THE ANGEL'S LAIR

Doc Savage and his men never did know just how long the trip in the submarine required. Doc probably could have given a very close estimate, but the nearest he ever actually came to setting a time was, "Several days." Monk insisted it was a year.

Monk was having a very tough time indeed. Not only was he unable to convince his captors he was not a financial sharper, but he had to perform all kinds of menial tasks—washing the dishes, washing clothes, wiping the engines. He had to get down on his knees when Nat Piper, Boscoe or any of the others passed. If he did not, he was promptly knocked down. To be sure, he retaliated by knocking down a man now and then himself, but it was small satisfaction.

Monk was further troubled by his fellow prisoner, old Leander Quietman. The old man was slowly turning into a fiend. Or perhaps the fiend had been there all the time and was just beginning to show himself.

At any rate, old Quietman was no individual to have for a fellow prisoner. Not the least of the difficulties was the way old Quietman had taken to talking in his sleep. He did not mumble words which could not be understood, as do most sleep talkers. What he said was distinct.

It curled Monk's hair. Old Quietman talked about the men he had swindled, men he had ruined, driven to their graves. And old Quietman gloated about it. Actually slavered his joy. It made Monk shudder.

Monk would give Quietman a resounding slap and wake him up. But the old reprobate would only go to sleep, and the talking would start again. During his waking hours, Quietman had taken to staring at Monk in such a fierce way that the homely chemist began to wonder if the hitherto supposedly benevolent old man had cannibal ideas. The bread-and-water diet was enough to give them to him.

Ham, when Monk complained audibly about his difficulty, only laughed gleefully.

Monk suggested to Piper that he, Monk, would willingly turn over his personal fortune to charity and reform forever if they would only let him drown Ham. The suggestion was not adopted.

The two pets, Habeas Corpus and Chemistry, were aboard, Monk had discovered. The two animals were permitted to remain in the company of Ham, Johnny, Long Tom and Renny.

Monk was not permitted to even pick his pig up and swing him by the ears, a process Habeas Corpus enjoyed. Furthermore, Habeas was getting distinctly fatter, and Monk was permitted to overhear talk indicating the shote would be turned into bacon as soon as a vote decided he would not be entirely a rind.

Little was heard from Doc Savage. Nat Piper and the others were very careful with the bronze man, giving him no chance to make a break.

Everyone was in a frame of mind to welcome the stopping of the engines when they finally did halt.

Before the machinery stopped, however, a mysterious process was followed. First, the Diesels were shut off. The electric motors started whining. These were used for underwater propulsion. The submarine went under water. Very slowly. Nat Piper shouted orders nervously. Two men were at submarine sounding devices.

Three times, the craft grated against something which sounded like rock. It was barely moving, and no harm was done.

Finally, it came to the surface and the motors were shut off.

Nap Piper came and grinned at Monk.

"We're here," he said.

NONE of the prisoners were permitted to go on deck and look at the surroundings for a while. Instead, Nat Piper had his men bringing more of the yoke-and-chain devices.

"I've been thinking," Piper told Doc Savage. "You and your men seem to have a bit more spirit than we like to see. You are our prisoners. You've got to understand that. And I'm afraid you don't. So we are going to take measures."

The measures seemed to be the application of a yoke to Doc and each of his men.

Only Nancy Quietman was spared.

"You'll go in with the rest of our patients," Nat Piper told Doc Savage and his men. "When we have decided you understand we are running this show, we'll ease up on you."

The bronze man made no comment, and the prisoners were escorted on deck. They stared about.

"Glory be!" homely Monk exploded. "How'd we get in this place without flyin'?"

It was big-fisted Renny who more closely described the way the place impressed them all.

"A cup," he said. "We're in a cup, or maybe you'd call it a hole. A devil of a hole."

That was about it. The walls were not high. Two hundred feet or so. But at least a hundred feet of that was sheer straight up and down. At one side, the wall was lower, and a sizable stream of water poured over the edge into the oval lake in which the submarine lay. But nowhere could a man climb the wall.

There was no visible outlet to this stream. But the prisoners knew there was an outlet. Underground. Leading to the sea. The submarine had come up it, submerged.

It was cold. Snow was visible in the crannies of the rocky cliff. The interior of the submarine had been warm, and those on its deck shivered. But the shudders were not entirely because of the cold. They had seen the repenting men. They had no way of knowing just yet that they were the repenting men. They found that out later.

The men had yokes, chains and leg irons. They were tall men, short men, fat men, thin men, old ones and young ones. They all wore rough khaki. They were all on their hands and knees on the shore. They were not looking at the submarine, but at the rocky, cold ground.

Not all the men wore yokes. Only twenty-two of them. The other men, about half a score of them, were green devils who stood around leaning on their forked spears.

"This gets nuttier and nuttier!" Monk exploded.

Monk referred, of course, to the green devils with the forked spears. The green devils were really men, but they were dressed in green devil outfits. Their forked spears had thick shafts. One incongruous touch was the tin military helmets they wore.

By now one of the submarine's dories had been gotten into the water, and the prisoners were ferried ashore and lined up with the other poor wretches who were yoked.

"GET down on your knees!" Nat Piper directed. "Hereafter, whenever a devil comes near you, you get down on all fours and pray for the deliverance of your soul and ask to be made a good man."

"I don't object to the praying," Monk declared. "But I'll be danged if I'll kowtow to them guys. Where'd they get them devil outfits anyhow?"

"From a musical comedy that went broke in New York," Nat Piper grinned. "We bought them. You may think it's a childish touch at first, but before long it becomes quite symbolic."

"Symbolic of what?" Monk snorted.

"Of the place where financial shysters go when they die," Nat Piper said. "Get down and bow!"

Monk, who was never bashful in the face of odds, waved his arms and managed to jump up and down bull-ape fashion in spite of his yoke.

"I'll fight all your devils first!" he yelled.

Renny roared, "And I'll help you!"

The green devils seemed to enjoy this. They grinned, held their forked spears ready and advanced.

The line of prisoners kept on their hands and knees, and watched. There was nothing but dejection on their faces.

Monk squared off. Renny followed suit. So did the rest of Doc's men. Doc, however, did not.

"You are only asking for trouble," the bronze man advised quietly.

Monk said, "Maybe, but I feel like asking for it."

One of the green Lucifers jumped at Monk. He poked the homely chemist lightly with his spear. Results were explosive. Monk howled, jumped high in the air, nearly broke his neck with the yoke, and came down flat on his back. He squalled, *"Ow! Oww—w!"*

"Holy cow!" Renny blared, having been prodded himself.

The would-be scrappers were speedily induced to get down on all fours.

"The spear handles contain batteries, spark coils and a push button," Nat Piper grinned. "They deliver an agonizing but harmless shock."

"We tried whips first," Boscoe added. "But these beat whips all hollow."

Nat Piper said solemnly, "Day by day, in every way, I want nothing more than to love my fellow man."

"What's that?" Monk gritted.

"It's what you say out loud every time a green devil passes you," Nat Piper explained. "Say it."

"I won't!" Monk yelled.

One of the unique spears poked him.

"Ow-w-w!" Monk roared. "Day by day, in every way, I want nothing more than to love my fellow man!"

The homely chemist scowled, then added, "And I do hope, to get a rope, and tie it snug, around the necks of you mugs!"

For that, they gave him an extra prodding with the electrical spears.

HAM was grinning. The whole thing struck him as so ridiculous as to be funny.

But some of Ham's amusement leaked when he was put to work with the yoked men. It seemed they were building a new barracks hut. The captives were engaged in shaping the stone blocks out of boulders. Each man was furnished with a small hammer for this purpose.

Monk, debating his chances of hitting the nearest green demon with his hammer, decided the fellows were wearing their incongruous soldier helmets as a defense against just that.

Doc Savage had apparently resigned himself to his fate. He went to work quietly and chipped out two very good stone blocks.

Nat Piper stood in the background, watched this, and was not pleased.

"Keep an eye on the bronze fellow," he warned his amazingly attired guards. "That bronze fellow is as full of tricks as he can be."

When they had their blocks completed, the prisoners were ordered to carry them toward the line of cliffs. They did so. They were stiff with the cold.

Then they saw the barracks. These were long stone huts, about as inviting to the eye as tombstones. Their location was behind a small rock ridge which stood some distance from the cliff. That was why they had not been seen from the water. The huts, however, were some distance from the cliff, too.

"We build 'em back a ways because pieces fall off the cliff during cold weather," Boscoe explained. "The cold splits off the rock somehow."

By the time dusk came, the prisoners were very tired. All afternoon they had found it necessary to work as fast as they could. Not entirely because of the green imps who stood around with their spears. It was cold. If one loafed, he almost froze.

It got colder with darkness. The prisoners were confined all in one long barracks hut. Considering that they were gentlemen in the process of being reformed, they did not behave themselves well. They stole each others' blankets. They snapped and snarled at each other. There were two fights.

Monk felt sorry for them until he awakened, stiff and blue with cold, and discovered some one had sniped the blankets off him while he slept. After the homely chemist staggered around and got himself able to walk again, he went hunting and came back with more than his share of blankets.

Monk rolled himself tightly in the blankets. The others were doing the same thing. It seemed to be necessary.

AT breakfast, Doc and Monk both tried to talk to their fellow prisoners. The results were not encouraging. They were snarled at impolitely unless they confined all their talk to one subject: the stock market. What was it doing? What were the quotations on this stock, that one? Was the government keeping its hands off?

One realization was necessary: These financial wolves were not being reformed. They were merely being goaded into showing their true natures. They were not suave slickers. They were vicious cutthroats.

Monk had never seen a set of gangsters who acted more like thugs.

"You were right, Doc," Monk said. "The Sea Angel is using the wrong system in trying to reform these eggs."

The rest of the day passed and brought nothing except a liberal education in the difference between a low criminal who uses a gun and a high one who uses his wits. The latter were more adept.

These men were the most skillful shirkers Monk had ever seen. They had formed themselves into small cliques, and these groups preyed on each other, stealing each other's food and extra garments, conniving to get the easy jobs.

The prisoners were supplied their food, which they had to cook themselves. When Monk got ready to cook his lunch, he found his food had disappeared. He squawked. The green devils told him that was his hard luck; they thought he had hid it himself to get a double ration. He would have to go hungry until the next day's ration was distributed.

That evening, all saw the Sea Angel.

THE eerie monster appeared and perched on the rim of the unscalable cliff which surrounded the bowl. It remained there for some time, motionless.

Nat Piper came out of his hut, looked at the creature. Then he waved.

The Sea Angel gestured slightly with one silver-hued flipper in return.

"Holy cow!" Renny told Doc. "I kinda figured up until now that Nat Piper was the Sea Angel. What do you think, Doc. Is the thing real?"

The bronze man did not reply.

The Sea Angel was still there when darkness fell.

Nancy Quietman seemed to be faring well enough. She had been assigned a small cabin to herself, but was not permitted to move about unless she was accompanied by a guard. The guarding job was one very much in demand.

The two pets, Habeas Corpus and Chemistry, had been taken in charge by the young woman. Monk was alarmed to note that Habeas seemed much fatter.

The next day, Doc Savage selected a strata of particularly hard stone on which to work. This rock, being of flint hardness, was avoided by the prisoners because it was very difficult to shape it into blocks.

Doc pounded away industriously.

About noon, he showed the green devils his hammer. The iron head of it had been beaten into a small knob on the hard rock.

They gave him another hammer. Then they made him work on rock which was not so hard on the hammers.

That evening, a wind moaned over the stone bowl. By dusk, snow was falling. Cold snow. It funneled over the edges of the bowl like sugar.

Nat Piper made the rounds, warning, "Do not leave your huts to-night. You might freeze."

Flannel rags were given the prisoners to wrap around the iron yokes so the cold metal would not touch their necks.

Piper spoke to Doc Savage. "Percy Smalling usually keeps in touch with us through a twenty-meter radio amateur station. We haven't been able to contact him. Did you do something to him?"

"No," Doc said.

Nat Piper seemed to believe the bronze man. He scratched

his head. "I wonder if H. O. G. Coolins got him. I'm afraid I'll have to sail the submarine back to New York to investigate."

Piper grinned. "We're going to get a politician next. He's been swiping the public money appropriated to relief."

Doc queried, "Does Percy Smalling know the location of this spot?"

"He has the latitude and longitude of this spot on the coast of Iceland," Nat Piper said.

Doc Savage was careful to look as if he was glad to know they were on the coast of Iceland. As a matter of fact, they weren't. Doc knew that. Iceland has a certain type of rock formation, and this wasn't that type.

This was Labrador stone. North Labrador, on the east coast of Canada. The bronze man had not neglected geology in his studies.

Nat Piper left, looking worried.

Other nights had been quiet. This one was noisy with the howl of the blizzard. Doc had been waiting for a noisy night, and he went to work.

FROM the cuff of his khaki coveralls—the garments had no pockets—the bronze man drew several small slivers of steel. These were crescent-shaped, and thin.

They had come off the head of the hammer Doc had ruined. To form them was his purpose in working on the hard stone everybody else had shunned.

The slivers were not good lock-picking instruments. But then the locks on the leg irons were not particularly complicated. In something like ten minutes, Doc got them off.

The bronze man pushed out into the howling blizzard and looked around. There were no guards patrolling in the blizzard. That, however, did not mean safety.

Doc had been using his eyes. This place was wired with a hidden alarm system. Buried plates and wires which, if a man walked near them, had their capacity increased enough to actuate a delicate relay.

The bronze man watched the cliff rim. The snow purled over steadily. It formed little overhanging ledges of drift. These grew larger. Directly, one of them came loose and fell. Two or three hundred pounds of damp snow.

Doc remained where he was. He saw snow fall in lumps three different times.

The bronze man was satisfied. That snow, falling in chunks,

would operate the capacity-system burglar alarms, the same as a man walking over the plates or near the wires. Nat Piper's men would probably have the alarms shut off.

Doc went back and picked the leg-manacle locks of his men. This aroused the other prisoners. Immediately, they all demanded to be turned loose.

"We'll kill Piper and all his men!" an old gentleman snarled.

That was exactly what Doc had expected. It was the reason he did not want to free them yet. The bronze man did some explaining intended to placate them.

Doc described the horrors and hardships of an escape most realistically. He explained that whoever escaped would send back a rescue party, and those who remained behind to be rescued would really have the easiest time of it. This appealed to these unfortunate financial wolves. They quieted down.

Doc Savage and his men now had the leg manacles off, but they still wore the yokes.

"I don't know how we're gonna get rid of these," said Monk, who had immense strength in his arms. "I tried to spread mine until I was blue in the face. I couldn't budge it."

"Lie down," Doc directed.

Monk did so. Doc put his feet in one side of the yoke. He fastened the leg irons of his own yoke to the other side of Monk's yoke. Then he straightened, used all of his tremendous strength, Monk grinned and got out of his yoke as it spread.

"A little help with mine," Doc suggested.

Both Monk and Renny, the two strongest of Doc's aids, added their sinew effort to that of the bronze man. He got his yoke off. They freed the others.

Monk dry-washed his hands and squeaked, "I'm ready to go to town!"

Chapter XIX

DEATH RENDEZVOUS

THE bronze man and his aids left the long barracks hut.

"Walk straight for the cliff," Doc suggested.

That was so they could circle the strange hide-out and approach the submarine from the opposite side. All had trouble with the falling snow. Once, they were completely buried for a time, but extricated themselves.

Doc and his aids did not begrudge the snow. It would render the alarms ineffective.

They reached the edge of the water, moved along it. The snow was knee deep. It got up their trouser legs. Their clothing was thin. Monk had to hold his jaw to keep the clatter of his teeth down.

The small wharf where the submarine dory commonly docked loomed.

"Br-r-r!" Renny gulped softly. "They've got the dory aboard the sub."

"We'll have to swim out," Ham said.

Monk gave a great shake and said, "I'll give myself up before I'll do that! There's ice around the edges of this salt water. And when salt water freezes, it's cold!"

Doc Savage slid out of his bulky coveralls. This left only his shorts.

"Keep moving so as not to get stiff," he directed, and waded quietly into the water.

The water felt warmer than the air at first. Then much colder. The bottom was of rock. With his hands, the bronze man pushed aside the slush ice. He took long, easy strokes, keeping his arm beneath the surface, using a submerged beat kick. He made good time.

The submarine was a hard, slimy mass. Snow coated the plates, was a mush in the water. The steel was slick, Doc worked to the bow, maneuvered carefully and got aboard. Shape of the submarine made it more difficult at the bow, but he had a reason for picking that point.

He was right. There was a lookout in the conning tower. But the fellow had crouched down out of the blizzard, and could not see the bow.

The fellow was dozing. Snow had stuck to the bronze man's damp skin. It was a silent, white ghost who descended upon the lookout.

Doc's metallic fingers found the fellow's spinal nerve centers and did something which only his vast knowledge of anatomy made possible. Pressure induced a strange paralysis. The victim was conscious, but could not move or cry out. He had made no sound.

Doc listened. No sound. The conning-tower hatch was open for ventilation. The bronze man descended quietly. It was warm below. Snow melted and ran off the big, metallic-looking man. A single electric bulb glowed. The blizzard sounded far off, and somewhere forward an ordinary alarm clock ticked noisily.

Doc made for the clock ticking.

Six men were aboard. All were in the large sleeping compartment. Their clothes and their weapons hung from hooks.

After he had made sure all were asleep, Doc collected the weapons. Then he silently closed the compartment doors and dogged them shut. He twisted the metal dogs down, using most of his strength. After that, the chances were none of them would be able to free them without the aid of hammers. And there would be no time to use hammers.

Doc started in on the sleepers.

TWICE, his luck was very good. The first two men fell victims of the nerve center paralysis as quietly as had the lookout on deck.

The third man must have been having a tense dream. At the touch of the bronze man's fingers, the fellow emitted an ear-splitting squawl. It aroused the others. They rolled out of their bunks.

Doc tightened down on the one who had howled. Inducing the nerve paralysis required a second or two. Doc held on. The other four men rolled out of their bunks and sprang upon the bronze giant

One man seized a pair of trousers. Doc ducked him twice. The third time, the fellow got the trousers around the bronze man's neck. He held on, twisted the two ends together, tightened down.

"Help me!" he croaked. "This is our only chance!"

Two of them held the improvised garrot. The third man was now paralyzed. The fourth survivor sprang back, wrenched up a floor plate. This exposed the batteries. Also a shiny, mechanical gadget—a float and an electrical contact device. The man jerked the float.

On deck and in the control room, sirens began howling.

Doc had not known about that. It was a patent bilge alarm. It warned of water high enough to endanger the batteries. The man had thought quickly and set it in operation.

Having done his good deed, the fellow sprang back to the attack. Doc met him with a fist. The fellow looked startled, foolish, sat down and took his jaw in both hands.

The other two men were tough. They knew their way around in rough-and-tumble. Their fists found sensitive places. Their kicks hurt. They were hard to hit.

Over and over, the two went. The choking trousers were still around Doc's neck. Very tight, now.

The two sirens still moaned alarmingly.

Doc trapped one foe with his legs. The fellow said, *"Oo-s-h!"* as his air went out. He released the trousers. Doc twisted, got free of the other man. The fellow leaped for the bulkhead door, fought the dogs.

With just the right force to make unconsciousness without undue damage, Doc bumped the other man's head on the iron floor. The fellow, when released, rolled over and lay half in the battery tray.

The last man squared off and tried to box, which was his mistake, because there was a loud report and it was some time before he awakened.

Doc hauled the man out of the battery tray so the acid on top of the storage batteries would not eat his hands.

Then the bronze man jerked the bilge alarm contact open. The sirens stopped. Too late, probably.

It was too late. Doc saw that when he reached the conning tower.

Nat Piper had heard the siren alarm. The whole interior of the rocky pit was white with light from a flare which he had put out.

PIPER's men were running for the water. Three of them carried light skin kayaks. Eskimo-type boats.

Monk and Doc's other aids had hesitated about entering the

water. They were cold. The water was cold. It was doubtful if they could all make it to the submarine, swimming. But they had decided to try.

There was no shooting. Merely action. Piper's men raced to the water, launched their kayaks. Some one put out a second magnesium flare and made things brighter. A weird scene with the snow, the wind and the fast movement.

Ham was in trouble now. A cramp from the cold. He cried out once and sank. Monk, who had frequently voiced the hope Ham would drown, turned back and helped him.

Doc raced forward, worked with the dories, endeavoring to get one in the water. The submarine was anchored. Getting the hook up would take time.

Launching a dory would take too much time, too. They were collapsible craft. Work with a wrench was necessary to make them water-tight.

Doc whipped back to the tower, went below. He got some of the guns he had collected. He broke them, looked at the cartridges. At first glance, they had the appearance of blanks. But tiny print on the wads said, "Reg. Tear." Tear gas. No good here. He looked. There seemed to be no cartridges with bullets.

He went on deck and plunged overboard. The water felt like solid ice, full of needles. And it was too late, anyway. Nat Piper's men in the kayaks had overhauled the swimmers. The latter dived.

Piper's men began tossing grenades into the water. They threw them well clear of the swimmers, so that the terrific concussion as they exploded would show the swimmers they had no chance.

Monk and the others realized this. They permitted themselves to be hauled ashore.

The three kayaks raced Doc for the undersea boat. The bronze man beat them, but by no more than twenty feet.

He pitched into the conning tower, dropped the senseless lookout below, followed, snapped down the hatch, made it snug. Then he sprang to the controls and sank the submarine.

Nat Piper's men stamped the deck and swore as the U-boat submerged. Then they were washed off and could only swim.

WATER in the cup was deeper than expected. Fully a hundred feet. Doc brought the craft to rest gently on the bottom. There were several things to do in order to make the craft safe, and he did them, then conducted a leisurely search of the craft. He was safe here for the time being, for Nat Piper was not likely to endanger his craft and his own men, even if he did become bloodthirsty.

Doc found several of the all-enclosing rubber gas suits. He located grenades. But none of the gas. He tied the prisoners, but did not gag them.

The prisoners awakened, and after they had a good swear, took it philosophically.

"You can't buck the Sea Angel," one said, grimly.

"You're not up against anything human with the Sea Angel," another said. "Yeah, you're out of luck."

Doc did not remark what he thought either way. He went into the control room and stationed himself at the sensitive underwater sounding device. This functioned by registering the intervals a sound took to reach the bottom of the sea and be reflected back.

But it was also a device which picked up any underwater sounds.

The bronze man heard small noises almost at once. Then he was aware of a scraping aft. He knew what that meant. The rubber suits. They were diving rigs as well as gas protection. Nat Piper's men had dragged a cable out of the submersible and were fastening it to the craft.

Whipping to the controls, Doc blew the tanks. The undersea boat came to the surface with a rush, and the bronze man flung the conning-tower trap open. He got outside with his hands full of the grenades.

Two kayaks were near by, where they had been overturned by the unexpected rise of the submarine.

Doc flung a grenade. It exploded far off.

"Keep away!" his powerful voice crashed.

The men righted their kayaks expertly and paddled away.

Doc flung more grenades as a warning to the divers. After a while, the divers walked out on shore, removed their hoods and shook their fists at the submarine.

"Want to make a deal?" Doc called.

"Yes!" Nat Piper called. "Give yourself up and you won't get hurt!"

Doc did not answer to that.

Toward dawn, it stopped snowing.

And shortly after dawn, three big tri-motored planes scooted overhead. Their motors made a great bedlam. The rock cup reverberated like the interior of a drum.

The planes went on. In three or four minutes, they were back.

A door of one of the craft opened. An object tumbled through and fell toward the submarine.

It was poor Percy Smalling. He was alive when he was thrown out. He hit the water not a score of feet from the submarine.

Chapter XX

H. O. G.

THE planes arched over, stood on their noses, twisted from side to side. Machine-gun snouts bled red. One of Nat Piper's men was sickled off above the waist. The others ran, gained the stone huts.

Jacketed lead drummed the submarine plates, bubbled the water alongside. Doc went overboard. Not hit. He was after poor Percy Smalling.

Smalling had gone down. He was still below. Doc reached him, fifteen feet or so beneath the surface. The body was rag limp.

Doc used all the care he could, got it aboard. There was still life. A small thing, miraculously lurking in broken bone and mangled flesh.

Doc spread Smalling out on the catnap bunk in the control room. Really a locker with a pad thrown over it. Then Doc worked over the mangled man.

The planes came back and the machine guns cackled like iron things of death. Five- and six-bullet bursts slammed the deck. Men who know machine guns and how they will heat and jam do not fire long bursts. Long bursts make aiming difficult, too.

Doc paid no attention. Percy Smalling might live. A miracle. His back was not broken. His skull was intact. Nothing much else about him was, though.

It was Coolins's gang in the planes, of course. Doc worked. The bronze man was skilled at many things, but first he was a surgeon. The submersible's medicine cabinet furnished some of the tools of the trade. Judging from the cabinet, one of Nat Piper's men was a surgeon.

THE opiate to ease Smalling's pain also started him talking. His lungs were not punctured. Doc did not try to stop him talking. Smalling was rational, almost.

"They tortured me," he said. "I had to tell them something."

97

I told them this place was in Iceland. They thought it was in Iceland, anyway. We make all our patients think that."

He shut his eyes, and the crushed pulp of his face worked.

"We hunted along the Iceland coast for a week," he creaked. "Then they knew I was lying. They kept torturing me. I didn't talk. Not willingly. But they gave me some stuff. I think it was a truth serum. They got it out of me—I didn't want—couldn't help——Oh-h-h-h!"

Smalling shut his eyes again. He seemed dead.

Then he said, "My pocket—note——"

He did not talk any more. But he was not dead.

Doc read the note:

NAT PIPER:
  We want your submarine, your base and your prisoners.
  We want the Sea Angel dead.
  We don't care about the rest of you. You may leave.

It was printed and not signed.

"Coolins?" Doc Savage asked.

Percy Smalling, who looked as if he were dead, emitted a small sigh that was "Yes."

"What does Coolins want with the prisoners?" Doc queried.

"Ransom," Percy Smalling managed, after a long while. "They are all wealthy men. Millionaires. We only got the big crooks. They can pay ransom. Millions—can—will——"

He shut his eyes. Kept them shut, rather.

"Open your eyes," Doc directed.

Smalling opened them.

Doc held the bright lens of a flashlight in front of the man's face, not shining it into his eyes, but so he could see its brightness.

"Hope," the bronze man said in a calm, firm tone. "All men have it. All men can keep it. You can keep it. You must keep it. While you have it, you will go on and on."

The bronze man talked slowly and distinctly. With his finger tips, he helped poor Percy Smalling keep his eyes open. His voice was an encouraging, an inspiring and powerful thing.

He extinguished the light.

"You still see it," Doc said. "You have it in you. Hope. You will keep it. You will live. While a man has hope, he will not die. You will keep yours and live. Keep it. Keep it——"

After a while, Percy Smalling was hypnotized, and held in his subconscious, pain-racked mind the will to go on living.

The thing which would do more than anything else to make him hold to the thread of life.

Doc Savage had done this sort of thing before. It was not exactly new. The power of hypnotism, if properly used, has long been recognized.

Doc took the note, a monkey wrench, some string, and went up onto the conning-tower platform.

THE planes had gone away. But not their sound. They were off to the west, out of sight. Their noise indicated they were seeking a landing place—finding it, too.

Nat Piper, Boscoe and the others had come out of their stone huts. They were rigging a machine gun. Their silence was grim.

Doc called, "Coolins!"

"The H. O. G.," Nat Piper barked back grimly.

"You're in a jam," Doc said.

"I can clean my own fish," Piper said.

"Catch," Doc directed.

The bronze man set himself on the fore-deck grating, drew back and threw the monkey wrench, to which he had tied the note with the string. It looked like an impossible throw. But the wrench arched up, made it. The note was knocked off when the wrench hit shore rock, but was not torn so badly but that Nat Piper and Boscoe could read it.

"This don't tell me anything," Nat Piper called. "I guessed it already."

Doc said, "Come aboard. Unarmed. Bring the prisoners. I will open the forward compartment, and you will file in there and I will lock you in. We'll get away before they come back."

"What about me?"

"You are a mental case, yourself," Doc Savage said. "You are possessed of a mania for punishing wealth. You were swindled once yourself, weren't you?"

"Yes!" Nat Piper said, with emotion. "I was ruined. Every cent taken from me. This is my revenge."

"It upset your mental balance," Doc said. "You need treatment."

"I'm not crazy!"

"Not insane, no. But you will admit there is something twisted in a mind that will conceive a scheme as wild as this whole thing."

Nat Piper got mad. He did not like being advised that he was not exactly balanced.

"I suppose you can cure me!" he yelled wrathfully.

"I maintain an institution that will do it," Doc replied.

Nat Piper snorted loudly. "What about the Sea Angel?"

Doc did not reply immediately.

"You and I know what the Sea Angel is," he said.

This obviously startled Nat Piper, because he absently rubbed his jaw and looked at his feet, then behind him at the largest of the huts, the one which he and his men occupied.

"Damned if I surrender!" he yelled. "I'll fight you and Coolins both!"

Doc had expected as much. A young man who had done the things Nat Piper had done, fantastic as they were, would not give up until the last ditch.

Doc gave some advice.

"Get all the prisoners but my men in the open and chain them on the far side of the bowl," the bronze man advised. "Coolins will not harm them, because they mean money to him."

Nat Piper nodded. "Good idea."

"Hide my men," Doc directed. "Otherwise, Coolins will kill them."

"Fat lot of hell I care about your men!" Nat Piper yelled, still smarting about the reflection on his mental balance.

But he kept Doc's five aids under cover.

Coolin's came before long. His men dropped a few bullets into the stone bowl to get attention. Nat Piper and his men scudded to shelter.

"Have you decided to give up?" Coolins bawled.

No one answered him.

"We'll lower a rope ladder down the cliff!" Coolins roared. "Climb it with your men!"

There was a stir at the large hut. The door opened. In the aperture appeared a gleaming gray hulk. It squirmed, got through the door and became the weird shape of the Sea Angel.

The thing straightened and absently folded its wings, flinging the long, black tendrils over its back. The creature had a certain dignity.

A rifle whanged. The bullet struck the Sea Angel. There was not the slightest doubt of it. Struck, and glanced off! The bullet made a bumblebee whizz going off into the sky.

The Sea Angel turned, stalked to the hut door, and calmly entered. When it had vanished, the door closed, but opened almost immediately to let Nat Piper shove his head out.

"You see!" Piper yelled. "You're not fighting men alone!"

A rifle bullet went *s-slack!* into the door beside his head. He ducked back.

"We'll take our chances with that thing, too!" H. O. G. Coolins roared.

Two bullets tapped the submarine conning tower where Doc was watching, and he got down quickly. Repairing to the control room, the bronze man used the periscope.

Coolins's men tried to throw grenades onto the roofs of the huts. They had no luck. The huts were located too far from the base of the cliff and, although it seems otherwise, it is impossible for a man to throw an object from a height a great deal farther than he can throw it on level ground.

Rifle fire was sporadic. Piper's gang did not show themselves. Neither did Coolin's gang—after one of them was shot unexpectedly by some one in the huts below.

Nat Piper's men had started killing in self-defense. It was, as far as Doc knew, the first life they had taken.

With strings and bits of leather, Coolin's men fashioned slingshots. The kind of weapons with which David slew Goliath. They tried launching the grenades with these. Their luck was not admirable. After they nearly blew themselves up, they quit that. They withdrew. Strange, tapping sounds became audible.

One of the planes flew over that afternoon. Nat Piper, Boscoe and some others peppered it with bullets. The plane did not come back, which was wise. Its cabin was not armored. The one bomb it dropped did not damage the huts much. The tapping back of the cliff continued monotonously.

Doc Savage worked over Percy Smalling, renewing the wound dressings and the hypnotic spell.

The bronze man's afternoon was almost without other incident, except that they shot the lens out of his periscope, rendering it useless.

The night, when it came, was so full of moonlight as to be like day.

Doc Savage studied the night sky for a time, and if he was disappointed because it was not dark, it did not show on his smooth, metallic features. He went below and examined the machinery, the fuel tanks, and made certain adjustments with valves.

In the conning tower again, but sheltered from bullets by the steel rim, the bronze man called out loudly. Power and volume of his trained voice echoed off the cliffs.

Doc spoke Mayan, the ancient lost language which few besides himself and his men could understand.

"Are you safe?" he demanded in the language. Back of the cliff the tapping stopped.

Monk bawled from one of the huts, "So far!"

"Tied?"

"We sure are. What is your plan, Doc?"

"The wind is dropping," the bronze man said, in Mayan. "In an hour or so, there should be practically no breeze. Be ready for action then."

Monk did not reply to that. Renny tried to, but it was evident from the way his shout stopped that Nat Piper's men were gagging the prisoners. The tapping back of the cliff started again.

Nat Piper was scared. It showed in his angry shout.

"Savage!" he screamed. "I'm in too tight a spot to stand for any trouble from you! The first move you make, I'll have your men shot!"

Doc did not reply.

The twenty-two rich Wall Street men whom Nat Piper had been holding prisoner now set up a great yelling. They conveyed advice to H. O. G. Coolins. They told him how Nat Piper had his men distributed. They thought Coolins was there to help them.

Nat Piper roared at them, telling them the truth. The prisoners fell silent, not because they believed Piper, but because he promised to shoot them if they didn't shut up.

The moonlight got brighter, and the wind fell. The surface of the water inside the bowl became glass-smooth.

Doc Savage threw an empty, air-tight syrup bucket overboard. The spot against the east edge of the cliff, where it drifted, showed him the location of the subterranean outlet.

Nat Piper and Coolins both saw the bucket incident. It made them both uneasy. The tapping stopped again. This time, for good.

For a while, there was ominous quiet. The water falling down the cliff into the bowl did not make much noise. Hardly any of the snow had melted during the day. In the far-off, a pack of wolves howled. Twice, the owls made noise.

Doc dampened a finger and held it up. It got equally cold

all around. The wind had died completely. The bronze man was ready to go into action.

But so was H. O. G. Coolins.

IT wasn't exactly an explosion. It was more of a giant, abrupt moan. And a convulsion of the earth. The whole surface of the lake writhed and trembled from the shock. The submarine rolled slightly.

And meantime, a great section of the cliff toppled over, coming apart as it tipped, as if it were a brick wall; a giant wall made of bricks without mortar to hold them together. It roared as it came down. Dust blew up. The earth shook. It kept roaring a long time after it seemed the cliff should have all fallen at that one point.

Coolins's men, of course, had planted TNT or dynamite. The tapping sounds had been made as they had drilled.

When the dust cleared, the cliff was merely a steep slope of broken rock. A very steep slope.

Coolins's men came down. They moved carefully, so as not to dislodge the loose rock. The stones looked small from where Doc was, until he compared them to the size of the men descending. Then the rocks became big. Many of them larger than automobiles.

Nat Piper yelled. His men fired.

"Don't break out the gas!" Piper shrieked.

That was because he had seen H. O. G. Coolins's men were wearing rubber suits which would protect them from the gas. Coolins had come well prepared.

It was not likely many of Coolins's men would be hit. The big rocks of the steep debris slope sheltered them.

Doc went below in the submarine. The men he had overpowered in taking the undersea boat lay on bunks. White, tense. They knew what was happening, or most of it. Doc told them the rest in a few words.

Then he turned them loose. He gave them their guns loaded with tear gas.

"You can go ashore and fight," the bronze man said. "But Nat Piper has started using real bullets in his guns."

"I was afraid it would come to that," one of the men said quietly.

The men went out on deck. Bullets rapped about them. One man went down, his leg broken.

Doc changed his mind. "You cannot make it ashore. Stay here."

Then he told them something else that they should do.

After he had instructed them, the bronze man went overboard quickly.

THE cold water, so cold that it felt solid, gripped Doc like a hard animal. As if by pressure, it strove to paralyze his muscles.

Beneath the surface, he swam as far as he could. It was not more than half as far as he could normally have managed. He came up, was shot at, got his lungs full of air, went down again. Three times Doc did that, and then the stone of the steep beach was underfoot.

Lunging, he got behind a boulder. From that to another. A fleeting, bronze ghost, almost naked, a strange figure in the snow, the bitter cold and the turmoil of men trying to kill each other.

The bronze man looked back at the boat. The moon was still bright, but the submarine seemed to lie in the middle of an ominous, black shadow upon the water.

Doc located the hut holding his men. He ran, dodged, crawled in the snow some of the time. And finally he reached the hut. The door was open. He went in. There was moonlight enough to see.

A man was stooping above Doc's aids. The man had a knife, and his face was set, grim. The prisoners were kicking madly at him.

Doc went in quietly. The man with the knife failed to notice the shadow for a moment, then realized there had been one. He turned, started violently.

He handed Doc the knife.

"You cut them loose," he said. "They seem to think I want to kill them. They keep kicking at me."

Doc took the knife. The man picked the gag off Renny.

"Holy cow!" the big-fisted engineer croaked.

The man who had had the knife said, "Piper said to cut them loose so they would have had a chance."

Doc slashed Monk's bonds. Monk removed his own gag and got up.

"That guy Piper has some good points along with his bad ones," the homely chemist grunted.

The prisoners got loose and got up and wheeled their arms around their heads and jumped up and down. Loosening muscles.

"If we only had something to fight with!" Ham snapped.

The man who had brought the knife began taking revolvers out of his pockets. He had several.

"Piper sent these." he said.

Doc Savage went to the hut door.

Coolins's men, some of them, were down in the cup. They fought cautiously, sure of themselves, of their superior numbers. They came on, as impossible to stop as a flood.

But Doc was interested in the submarine. The great black shadow around the craft had spread. It covered more than half of the inlet.

"Fire it!" the bronze man called loudly.

Those on the submarine heard. A brand of oil-soaked cloth, blazing with flames, arched out of the conning-tower hatch. The hatch then banged while the brand was still in the air.

Oil was on the water. Thick, but inflammable fuel oil. It caught fire. With a *whoosh!* it spread. Not as fast as gasoline, but fast enough.

The burning area grew. Pumps inside the submersible were still forcing out fuel oil. Thousands of gallons.

Burning fuel oil throws off almost as black smoke as any ordinary burning substance. The sepia pall grew, spread, tumbling and expanding. There was no wind to lift it out of the cup. It began to fill the place.

"That," Monk barked, "is what I call an idea!"

"Wait," Doc said, and the group waited.

The smoke wad grew, crawled toward them like an impossible black mushroom.

"The flames will not harm the submarine through her plates," Doc said, in case any one was worrying about that.

The smoke was almost on them.

"The men on the U-boat did this at my instruction," the bronze man explained.

The party sucked the first smoke into their lungs.

"Now," Doc said.

They ran toward the huts where Nat Piper and his gang were confined.

Coolins was yelling on the cliff. "Hold it!" he was bawling. "Hold it! They know the ground! You won't have a chance if you can't see anything!"

Maybe his men heard him. Perhaps they did not, and used their own judgment. They held their positions, firing a lot.

Doc and others kept down. They gained the thick-walled stone hut where Piper was barricaded.

"Piper!" Doc called, so he would not shoot them.

Piper, coughing, gritted. "Damn you! What do you mean by setting this smoke off——"

"Move fast," Doc said. "We have a chance to make the submarine."

Nat Piper did not have to think that over long.

"Come on, fellows," he said. "It may be an idea at that."

They came out. It was impossible to see one another or anything else in the darkness.

"I'll keep talking," Doc Savage said. "Follow my voice."

"Right."

"Over this way," the bronze man said, talking. "Keep close together and keep down, and do not fire back at those men. They are making so much noise with their shooting that they may not hear us. Keep down. Do not make any noise. We are going to pick up the prisoners. They are just ahead."

"You're going to take my rich men?" Nat Piper asked, and laughed queerly, almost madly.

Doc Savage said, "We will take them, of course. Although there is not much choice between you and Coolins in their case. They might even be better off in Coolins's hands."

He kept his voice low. It did not carry far. But it was full of a quality that made it easy to locate in the black pall of smoke. Voices can be made that way.

"Coolins would turn them loose, after they paid off. They would probably prefer that. Here they are."

Doc had found the first of the financial sharpers. They were still yoked, wore their leg irons. They were held together by a long chain which was fastened to a huge boulder.

"I left the key to this chain in the hut!" Nat Piper croaked suddenly.

Chapter XXI

TRAPPED BELOW

MONK said, "Blazes! Go back and get it!"

"Wait," Doc suggested. "Let's try something first."

The bronze man tested the weight of the boulder to which the chain was attached. It did not budge. They all lent their shoulders. The rock held its place. It weighed several tons.

Doc picked up the chain. It was heavy. He could never break it. He worked down to the lock. There was a chance there. He took two or three turns of the chain around each hand, then tossed a loop of it around his chest, over his arms, with the lock in the middle. He deflated his chest and slackened his muscles, then tightened the chain.

By this method, he could exert greatest strain. The force with which the human chest can expand is astounding, and the bronze man's muscles were tremendous. Every one held their breath.

The padlock broke.

The prisoners had been jumping about to limber their muscles. Some of them were reluctant about going along. To save argument, they were kept on the chain.

Doc began talking again, saying, "Follow my voice. The submarine is to move close to shore. Pick a spot where the water is deep. The oil will be burned off the water shortly. We should be able to get aboard."

"Help!" bawled one of the rich swindlers. "Help, Coolins! They're boarding the sub with us!"

Monk jumped and knocked the man senseless.

"Dumb-bell!" Ham told the homely chemist. "Now you can carry him."

Monk did so, grumbling. Two or three rifle bullets came toward the group. The smoke seemed to be lifting.

Coolins began howling. "Head them off, boys!"

Doc said, "Hurry up. Over this way. You can see each other now. There is the submarine."

The submersible had moved in, silent under its battery

power. The bow was aground. But twenty feet of water separated the bow from the beach, and flames were licking over the area. Small flames, but a man could not swim or wade through them.

"The boat," Doc called.

The men on the submarine had the dory ready. Red and blistered-looking, they first heaved a line ashore. Doc caught the end. Then the men tossed the dory bodily overboard. Doc and his aids pulled it ashore along the line.

Men loaded into it with some of the prisoners. They coughed, gagged in the smoke. Perspiration rolled. They got the first load onto the submarine.

Pretty Nancy Quietman was with the prisoners, her wrists handcuffed. She gasped when she touched the undersea boat's plates. They were evidently hot. Monk sprang aboard and lifted her onto the deck bodily. The plates were hot enough so that they had to keep dancing about.

The dory returned. Again. All the prisoners were aboard now, but Doc remained on shore, because it had been necessary for him to shove the hot dory to get it off.

Nat Piper held the other end of the line as Monk took the dory back for Doc.

And then Nat realized the position he held. He could throw the rope into the water and be free of Doc. The bronze man stood no chance of reaching the submarine. The nearly red-hot dory contained no oars. The water was aflame with burning oil.

Nat Piper coiled the rope and drew back to throw it away.

INSTEAD of throwing it, he said. "Oh, hell!" and pulled them to the submarine.

Monk gave him a parched grin. "I'll forgive you a lot for that."

Doc found the boat's plates hotter than he thought. The paint was off, naked red iron showing through in places. He kept in the air as much as possible, jumping aft.

Nancy Quietman eyed the bronze man anxiously as he dropped down the conning-tower companion.

"You're not hurt?" she wanted to know.

Her concern, considering the species of hell they had all been going through, was a bit surprising.

Doc said, "Have Monk take your handcuffs off in the engine room," gave her a brief expression that might have been a smile, and went to work.

The men got the conning tower hatch shut. It was hot, almost unbreathable in the submarine. There was not much smoke, however. The men had been careful to keep the hatch shut all they could.

The ballast tanks drank in water when the valves were opened. The submersible sank. The electric motors began to drone.

"Tail down," a man said. "That should lift the bow. Shall we back her off, sir?"

"Back her off," Doc said.

They backed, successfully. Doc watched the clock, the tachometer, judging the distance they had backed. The compass told him the direction.

"Kill sternway," he said.

The undersea boat lurched a little, stopped. The indicator said they were thirty feet down. It was not perceptibly cooler yet.

The prisoners, the rich men, were huddled around the control-room door. Some of them had been able to crowd into the passages with their yokes and were crouched there.

Nat Piper moved about to study the instrument panel. He had shoved his revolver into a hip pocket, but the grip projected.

One of the wealthy swindlers lunged suddenly, got the gun. He cocked it and crouched back, showing his lips, eyes ugly.

"Here's where *we* take a hand, damn you!" he croaked.

No one moved.

THEN Nancy Quietman came in, saying, "I just remembered. What became of the Sea Angel? We didn't see——"

She looked at the gun, which was now pointed at her. The handcuffs were not on her wrists. Monk must have removed them.

"Come over here, dear!" the man with the gun snarled.

The girl stood still.

The gun went off. Nancy Quietman screamed, dodged, fell.

"I'll kill you!" the man said. "Come over here!"

The girl had been startled, not hurt. She came over, trembling. The swindler with the gun got behind her.

The shot had drawn attention. Men rushed to the door. Old Leander L. Quietman was first, probably because he had been nearest the door. He still wore his yoke and chains.

Old Quietman crouched for a moment in the narrow bulkhead opening. His lips peeled off his teeth, and his face got a weird look.

He said something nobody could have understood. Just a gurgling in his throat.

Then he said, "That's swell. What do you want me to do?"

"Get their guns." The man using the girl for a shield nodded at Piper's men.

Old Quietman walked into the control room. But he walked toward the man with the gun.

"Don't be a fool!" Doc said to old Quietman.

Old Quietman seemed not to hear. His bloodshot eyes were fixed on the man with the gun. And the latter suddenly realized old Quietman was not with him. Quietman was going to attack him!

"Damn you!" he screamed.

Then the man pointed his gun at Quietman and pulled the trigger.

Doc jumped. He was in the air before the gun exploded. He hit it as it discharged, perhaps an instant before. The bullet missed Quietman, made a lead smear on the wall.

Doc's metallic fist took care of the man with the gun. Then Nancy Quietman clung to the bronze man and trembled. There was probably reason for the trembling, at least, and maybe for the other.

Old Quietman sat down weakly and grinned. It was a rather nice grin for such a wrinkled, old face.

"Funny," he said slowly. "I guess I'm quite an old louse, but she's the one thing—I love—I guess—I didn't care much whether he was going to shoot me."

Long, bony Johnny came bounding in, bumping his head everywhere, and barked, "I'll be superamalgamated! What happened?"

"A man got his conscience aroused," Nat Piper said dryly. "And I didn't think he had one."

"I didn't think so—either," old Quietman said, and laid over in a faint.

Doc Savage asked Nat Piper, "How do you follow the channel under the cliff to the sea? Sunken magnets?"

"How'd you guess?" Piper exploded.

"It is not a new method."

Piper walked to the lazybench—the single berth in the control room. He lifted the lid, and out of the locker exposed drew a box with sensitive meters.

"Turning a crank in this case lowers a feeler ball," he said. "It's an electrical contrivance which detects the presence of magnetism. The magnates on the bottom are heavy permanent magnets, and they——"

"We had better not waste too much time," Doc reminded.

Piper nodded. He reached into the locker and spun a crank which lowered a thin, perfectly round cable through a water-tight stuffing box. He watched the dial.

"Cruise back and forth," he suggested. "I'll pick up the line of magnets."

Doc gave orders. The motors whined and moved the submersible, and after a while, Piper said, "Now. Put her dead east."

The bronze man spun the wheel, careful to check the swing, and did a good job, bringing the compass indicator to rest less than a degree off the E on the dial.

"Slow," Piper said.

Doc asked, "How deep?"

"Six fathoms. The bowl is deeper than the entrance."

The submarine moved ahead, its speed a mile an hour perhaps. The tension grew. This was the critical test. If they got through, it would be simple to evade the planes.

Doc, to ease the tension, asked, "How did you happen to find this place the first time?"

"Gold mining was my business," Nat Piper said. "I prospected this coast years ago, and found this place. It was the season of the year when the tides are the lowest. When the tide is very low, you can see the underground mouth."

He took a breath. "The place fascinated me. I climbed down and camped in it."

"The cliff could be climbed, of course," Doc said, and it was a statement, not an inquiry.

"Yes. Starboard a bit."

Doc put her starboard a bit.

Nat Piper said, "You had to know where to climb the cliff. As I said, I remembered this place. And after I found this sub while cruising on a small ketch in the North Sea—I went around the world in the ketch after I was swindled out of my gold-mining company—I thought of this place and what an excellent spot it would be. Port a trifle."

Doc steered a shade to port.

"We're getting under the cliff," Nat Piper said. "I can tell. The magnets on the bottom are bigger under the cliff. We placed them with diving suits. Now—now—we're just getting under the ——"

What occurred next happened much too quietly. There was faint sound, barely audible over the motor whine. The submersible put its nose down.

Then there was a great grinding and rending of metal.

Doc whipped forward through the narrow bulkhead doors. He found men fighting the dogs at the bow compartment door. Water was sheeting in around the door as they fought to secure it. One of the men was fat, thieving Boscoe.

"The whole bow is crushed!" Boscoe said hoarsely.

Chapter XXII

FAST

DOC SAVAGE helped the men with the bulkhead door. They got it shut. But water still came in. About twenty gallons a minute. The door had been sprung.

The bronze man whipped back to the control room.

"It is not bad," he said.

That, perhaps, was misleading. True, they were alive. But they wouldn't be for long when that water got to the batteries. Salt water and the sulphuric acid in the batteries would combine to make a poisonous gas. More men have died in submarines from it than from anything else.

For that matter, gas had killed the original crew of the submarine. The Germans who had manned her during the World War.

The motors were in reverse, turning both propellers. They labored. Doc listened, watched. Nothing happened.

"We're fast!" Nat Piper croaked.

Two of the rich men he had been trying to reform promptly screamed like frightened children. One fainted.

Doc examined the instruments. The tanks had been blown completely in an effort to raise the boat. Nothing gained there.

"Coolins had rigged wires with weights on them, I'll bet," Nat Piper guessed irrelevantly. "The wires hung down into the water, and when the sub hit them, the jerk set off a mine he had arranged on the cliff."

"Or he decided to blast the cliff when we were under it," Monk suggested.

"One or the other," Nat Piper agreed.

They were a weird-looking crowd, black with soot, perspiring, faces anxious-looking. The rich men mumbled or moaned, and some, rather surprisingly, began to pray.

Nancy Quietman came to Doc Savage and rested a hand on his arm.

"Somehow," she said, "I don't feel as scared as I suppose I should."

The bronze man, not being entirely without perceptive powers, was by now aware that the young woman was showing rather more than casual interest. He was embarrassed.

Nancy Quietman was a very attractive bit of femininity, but that made it worse, because the bronze man made an unalterable practice of permitting himself no feminine entanglements. This was probably the only respect in which he forced himself to be not exactly human. It was not always easy.

Monk and Ham both perked up at this point. They were Doc's rescuers when something like this came up. It was their job to distract the pretty young woman's attention. Sure enough, Doc gave them the eye.

"Look," Ham suggested to Nancy Quietman. "Suppose you and I see what we can do toward reviving your grandfather."

"Of course," she agreed.

Doc turned his attention back to the instruments. He grasped valves and filled the tanks. The submarine settled, groaning a little.

"We only have air enough to blow the tanks once more," Nat Piper reminded him.

Doc seemed not to hear him. He ran the port propeller in forward speed, the starboard prop in reverse. The undersea boat groaned and moved a little again. Doc reversed the propellers. Another groan.

The bronze man did that several times. Then he reversed both wheels full speed. The U-boat moved.

"We're loose!" Nat Piper squawled.

HE lunged to blow the tanks and bring the submersible to the surface. Doc stopped him.

"But why not?" Nat Piper exploded.

Big-fisted Renny said, "Doc probably figures we'll need some foxy work to get out of this."

Doc Savage now gave orders to pump a large quantity of the fuel oil out into the water.

"It will rise to the surface and lead them to think we are down for good," he said. "Otherwise, they may try to set off depth bombs."

A man came from the forward compartment.

"The water is making gas from the batteries," he said. "I closed the next compartment. That will keep the gas out. Before long, there will be enough water in the boat so that we cannot get to the surface."

Doc Savage nodded, then looked at Nat Piper.

"The escape port aft works, does it not?"

"Yes," Nat Piper admitted. "A man can leave the submarine through it."

"You operate it," Doc directed. "Come on."

"But who's going out?"

Piper knew the answer to that when the bronze man entered the tiny barrel of a chamber which had a water-tight hatch at the bottom, and another hatch opening into the sea. Submarines, the more advanced ones, had been equipped with these during World War days. All modern undersea boats now have them.

Having examined the escape port, Doc dropped down and said, "Now, Piper, I want a true answer to my question."

Nat Piper took a deep breath. "You'll get it."

Doc asked his question.

"Where is the Sea Angel?"

Nat Piper swallowed, looked as if he wanted to lie, said, "I guess you want me to explain——"

"Where it is," Doc said.

"In the big hut," Nat Piper said.

Doc said, "Give me fifteen minutes. Then blow the tanks, bring the boat to the top and beach her."

Nat Piper swallowed. "Right."

Doc got into the escape port, closed the lower lid, and tightened it.

When the port was full, and the outer hatch wide, he swam out. He swam sidewise, and when increasing light told him he was near the surface, he was careful.

Smoke still hung over the water. But the fire had burned itself out. The new oil was thick. Doc got his head out and breathed.

A man was shouting on shore.

"There's fresh oil on the surface!" he was bellowing. "We've sunk the sub!"

Doc Savage sank quietly out of sight.

Chapter XXIII

THE ANGEL ON THE CLIFF

H. O. G. COOLINS, financial sharper who had not been re-formed, and who probably never would be, was torn between joy and disgust.

"We got them!" a man kept telling him. "We crushed the sub. That mine trap we fixed with wires got them."

Coolins swore.

"There's ten million dollars' worth of rich men in that sub-marine!" he snarled.

The man remembered that. And he began to swear, too. Coolins's other men heard the profanity, and thinking maybe some of their enemies had been discovered, came galloping around the edge of the bowl, close to the water.

Coolins swore at them, at himself, at everything.

"This is a hell of a way for things to turn out!" he said.

"It could have been worse," some one offered. "They could have licked us."

Meanwhile, the smoke was dissipating itself. It lifted slowly, and showed the greasy water in the bowl, the steep slope of the débris down which the men had made their charge, and the other features of destruction, including the bodies of some of Coolins's men who had been killed.

Among other things, the pig, Habeas Corpus, and the ape, Chemistry, were discovered. The two animals were lurking forlornly among the boulders.

A man said, "Let's make a clean sweep of it," and took a pot-shot at Habeas. He missed, because Habeas was hard to hit.

Another man said, "Suppose we search the huts and see if there was any loot left."

"What about the Sea Angel?"

That got silence. Uneasy quiet.

"There ain't been a sign of the thing," a man muttered.

Coolins gritted. "We've got to get the Sea Angel. Otherwise, we'll never be safe.

"Probably it was on the submarine," a man said.

"It can live underwater," some one reminded.

"And fly."

Then a man in the background croaked horribly, "Speaking of the devil——" He pointed.

"The Sea Angel!" Coolins bawled.

The weird monster had walked—if its queer, penguinlike progress could be called walking—out of the large hut. It seemed unaware that anything out of the ordinary had happened. Its progress was taking it toward the rock slide, by which it was possible for any one with legs to mount to the top of the cliff.

A man threw up his rifle, fired. He hit the Sea Angel. He was sure of it. But the thing merely jerked a little, and went on.

"After it!" Coolins roared.

Coolins's men held their rifles tightly and charged. They had quite a distance to go. The Sea Angel, weird creature, reached the rock slide and mounted rather rapidly.

Another man fired.

"No use shooting!" Coolins yelled. "Bullets won't touch it! You should know that by now!"

They panted as they ran.

"Then how—we gonna—stop it?" a man gulped.

"Grenades!" Coolins snapped. "I've got some grenades that will blow a battleship apart!"

The Sea Angel was almost halfway up the slide before the men reached the bottom. Coolins led his men, his face red. They scrambled up the precarious surface.

Several times, rocks were dislodged and threatened to start a slide. The whole slope was a precarious affair.

"It's—gaining!" Coolins groaned.

Some of his men were holding back. He discovered this, and it added to his rage.

"Come on, you fools!" he screeched. "We've got to get this thing!"

"I don't like that loose rock!" a man yelled.

Coolins, beyond caution, scrambled madly. He bit his lips until they ran red in his rage.

By the time he was halfway up the slope, the Sea Angel was only a few yards from the top.

The strange monster seemed to be looking back.

Coolins stopped. He dug one of his powerful grenades out of a pocket, drew back to throw.

An unexpected thing happened then. The Sea Angel spoke. "You're taking a chance!" it said.

Coolins wanted to take a chance. He was desperate, too mad to reason. He believed he could throw to the top, and if so, felt his grenade could blow the weird silver thing to bits.

Coolins threw the grenade.

He knew, an instant after he hurled the grenade, that he had overestimated his own throwing arm. It was going to fall short. Coolins leaped sidewise, trying to get out of the slide that was sure to follow the blast.

He did not make it.

The boulders came down, little ones the size of baseballs, and some as big as tractors. Hopping one over the other. Slithering and grinding and rubbing sparks.

They treated H. O. G. Coolins much as a grist mill treats a grain of corn.

Some of Coolins's men escaped the slide. Not all of them.

The submarine, coming to the surface about then, unloaded enough angry men to take care of the survivors. No one was killed in the process, miraculously.

A little while later, when Monk found a greasy spot on a rock, he swore up and down that he had found H. O. G. Coolins.

Monk, having disposed of that, and perceiving the weird form of the Sea Angel descending the newly reformed slide, dashed forward.

"I'm gonna go around and around with this thing until I find out what it is!" Monk gritted, and sprang upon the Sea Angel.

He was not shocked senseless by the long tendrils. He had, in fact, an easy time of it. There were some fastenings in the back of the creature. The chemist opened these.

"As Renny would say, 'Holy cow!' " Monk exploded.

He had uncovered Doc Savage.

THE bronze man got out of the rig, which was quite a complicated and heavy affair of aluminum beamlets supporting an amazingly light, considering its invulnerability, bulletproof covering. This was chain mesh in nature, several thickness, with padding between.

A man, once he had encased himself inside it, could navigate with fair agility. The weight was distributed so that the affair was not clumsy.

"But what gave them tendrils their kick?" Monk exploded.

Doc Savage showed him the extremely compact and powerful generator of high-frequency electric currents enclosed in the thing. This could be switched on to throw a charge into the long feelers when they were wielded.

"The same system the green devils used on their spears," Monk grinned.

A moment later, the homely chemist remembered. "But this Sea Angel flew. And it swam underwater."

Nat Piper came up and explained, "The thing you saw flying was a rubber imitation of this Sea Angel disguise filled with helium. One of my men released it from your penthouse. We were impressing you."

"How about the thing you showed us underwater?"

"Merely an affair of wood and luminous paint towed under the submarine," Nat Piper explained. "As for this bulletproof disguise here, we all took turns wearing it. First one, then another."

Monk looked into the disguise again. "Hah! Gas mask, too. That explains why gas didn't affect the Sea Angel. Some rig, but I feel kinda goofy about it. You know, for a while, I really thought this thing was something supernatural."

"They all did," Nat Piper said dryly. Then he looked at Doc Savage. "That is, but Savage, here," he added. "I suspect now that he guessed all along what it was."

Monk scratched his nubbin head. "But I don't see why all the elaborate business was necessary."

"Fear," Nat Piper said, and shrugged. "We felt a supernatural touch would add terror to our operations. Men are not scared of men. But men are scared of things they do not understand."

Which was logical reasoning.

Nat Piper, it developed, had suddenly decided to give up his project of trying to reform rich shysters by the methods he had been using. He had been doing some thinking, he explained a bit later, and he had concluded his methods were not getting very good results.

Which was just as well, because some of Doc's men had remained aboard the submarine to make sure Piper's men did not seize their prisoners again.

An expedition composed of Renny, Johnny and Long Tom discovered H. O. G. Coolins's three planes intact on a near-by bit of level country.

That took care of transportation back to civilization, although several trips would be necessary.

DOC SAVAGE and Nat Piper had a long discussion during the next two days, while preparations for departure were being made, and while Percy Smalling was getting well enough to be moved. Chemistry and Habeas had rejoined their masters.

It was agreed that Doc should take the "patients" which Nat Piper had not been making much progress with. The bronze man would put them through his institution for curing criminals by brain operations, which made them forget their pasts.

Old Leander Quietman was also sent to the institution, along with the others. After the wealthy men were trained to hate crime and crookedness, they would be allowed to go back to their fortunes.

The chances were very excellent that the men would then do a great deal of good with their money.

During this discussion, Monk was absent. Some one had stolen the jeweled collar of the pig, Habeas Corpus. Monk was wrathfully hunting the thief. He had a good idea of the latter's identity.

Ham seemed to be doing rather a good job of distracting pretty Nancy Quietman's attention from Doc Savage. Either Ham was very good, or the young woman had concluded the bronze man was impervious to pretty femininity.

Ham's success did not overly please Monk.

Monk was very mad when he appeared. He had the thief by the neck. The culprit was Boscoe.

Monk marched Boscoe up before Doc and ordered, "Speak your piece, sticky fingers!"

Boscoe swallowed a few times, then got it out.

"Look," he said. "Monk's been telling me about a place you got in up-State New York. Er—uh—Monk—I mean, I was wondering if you could take me there and cure me of being a thief?"